*A
Harlequin
Romance*

OTHER
Harlequin Romances
by GLADYS FULLBROOK

727—NURSES OF THE TOURIST SERVICE
771—NURSE PRUE IN CEYLON
899—ANN BELL, NURSING AIDE
1018—HOSPITAL IN THE TROPICS
1082—ARMY NURSE IN CYPRUS
1321—BUSH HOSPITAL
1346—A HOUSE CALLED KANGAROO
1412—JOURNEY OF ENCHANTMENT

Many of these titles are available at your local bookseller, or through the Harlequin Reader Service.

For a free catalogue listing all available Harlequin Romances, send your name and address to:

HARLEQUIN READER SERVICE,
M.P.O. Box 707, Niagara Falls, N.Y. 14302
Canadian address: Stratford, Ontario, Canada N5A 6W4

or use order coupon at back of book.

A HOUSE CALLED
KANGAROO

by

GLADYS FULLBROOK

HARLEQUIN BOOKS   TORONTO
WINNIPEG

First published in 1968 by Mills & Boon Limited,
50 Grafton Way, Fitzroy Square, London, England.

SBN 373-01346-9

Reprinted 1975

Printed in Canada

CHAPTER 1

SUSAN MANLEY walked slowly along Rundle Street in Adelaide, the capital of South Australia. The sun shone brightly down upon the crowds on the pavement, and her thoughts went back to the cold, fog-bound London streets which she had left behind her just a short three months ago. 'At the bottom and turn left', they had told her at the People's Palace in Pirie Street. She and Pat, the girl friend with whom Susan had emigrated to Australia, had been staying there for the last month; and it was this very morning that Pat had exploded the bomb-shell which had blown Susan's thoughts and plans for the future sky-high.

For Pat had told her that she was going to marry Jack Randall, who worked as a clerk in Dalgetty's, the big shipping firm in King William Street where she and Susan had obtained jobs in the typing pool. Susan had stared at her friend in wordless consterna-tion, for the news had seemed to her quite fantastic. Back home they had been typists in Croydon; Pat for four years, Susan for two. They had both agreed that being typists in a business firm in Croydon was not their idea of getting the best out of life. So, after some thought and a great deal of discussion, the two girls had decided to emigrate to Australia. Susan's mother had died some years previously and her father had recently remarried, and she had been feeling lonely and at a loose end for some time. Pat was one of a large loosely-knit family, and when she announced to them her decision to make a life for herself on the other side of the world, the rest of the family cheerfully told her that it was a good idea. So the two girls said their goodbyes and set off.

But they had not been living in Adelaide more than a couple of weeks before both girls were beginning to ask themselves why they had stopped being typists in Croydon just to become typists in Adelaide. Apart from the climate Adelaide was very much like any English country town; and as far as the job went—well, Susan had to tell herself sometimes that she really had left the job in Croydon and was here in Australia.

Not but what there were differences—big differences. There were the lovely sandy beaches, for instance; there was the sun which seemed to be always shining—and what else? Susan had now reached the corner of the street and glanced up at the buildings. Yes, here was Hindley Street where the kindly Salvation Army Major at the People's Palace had told her she would find the employment bureau. The People's Palace was really a huge hotel or hostel, and was run by the Salvation Army. Susan had heard that there were Palaces in nearly all the big towns throughout the country and that they were very popular. She could well believe that, for they were very cheap, the rooms and beds were clean and comfortable, and the food plain but good. Also, one met the most interesting—and sometimes the most extraordinary people. After the rather dreary lodgings out in one of the suburbs where they had gone on their arrival both girls were thoroughly enjoying staying at the People's Palace. It was there that they had met Jed, the horse-breaker from the Northern Territory, also Larry and Els, his wife, who were having a brief holiday from the opal mines in Coober Pedy. Then there were the two men, also on holiday from some isolated place near Cloncurry, who sat and watched television every evening in the big lounge, clad in rather grubby singlets, shapeless shorts, and with bare feet; and always with a couple of bottles of beer beside them on the floor. That at least was a change from Croydon, Susan thought; a smile crinkling the corners of her dark-lashed grey eyes. The fascination of the People's Palace was the fact that it had for the most part a floating population of weekly holidaymakers, so one was always meeting up with someone different.

But then, just as they had both decided that Adelaide was not their idea of Down-Under, Pat had met Jack Randall at the little dance hall at the corner of the street. She had gone there for the evening with another girl from the office instead of Susan because the latter had been invited by one of the Palace boys to go to see a travel film of Darwin and the Northern Territory at the Tourist Bureau in King William Street. Susan had thoroughly enjoyed her evening, and when she had enquired the next morning whether Pat had also had a good time the latter had positively glowed as she uttered a fervent 'yes!'

And that had been the beginning of it all. For after that evening Pat had been out with Jack at every opportunity, and the long and cosy discussions which she and Susan had had as to whether they would stay on for a time in Adelaide or make plans to move on somewhere else came to an abrupt end. Not that that worried Susan unduly, as she had by now made up her mind that she at least was not going to stay here in South Australia. This was not what she had come half-way across the world for. But even so, it had come as quite a shock when Pat had told her that she was going to marry Jack Randall. It was not that Susan had anything against Jack; he seemed a nice enough fellow, but—and here, at this point, Susan wondered uneasily if she would have come out here at all if she had foreseen this happening. It all seemed so sudden, and now, in a way, she felt very alone.

She was now walking slowly along Hindley Street, closely examining àll the signs and plates on walls, doors and in shop windows. Then—she spotted it. A brass plate on a doorway adjacent to a café kept by the almost inevitable Italian. The door was open and there was a narrow staircase with a pointing finger on the wall. Susan's heartbeats quickened as she hesitated for a moment and stared at the pointing finger. Should she go up? she wondered, with a sick sense of misgiving. After all, she was quite comfortable where she was at the Palace, and her job at Dalgetty's had prospects, so—but no, something urged her on, something which seemed to say: Go on, don't be afraid of pushing out alone into the unknown. Who knows what may be waiting for you there?

Quickly, but with slightly unsteady knees, Susan started up the stairs. At the top was a door with a white card pinned to it. 'Mr Caldwell', it said, 'Employment Exchange'. Hurriedly she knocked at the door before she could have another change of thought. A voice called 'Come in!'

A plump middle-aged man was sitting behind a

desk. He glanced at Susan as she advanced into the room, murmured a 'good morning' and waved her to a chair in front of the desk. She took a deep breath, sat down and waited. He finished writing something in a file, closed it briskly, then leaned back in his chair.

"Well—" he said, "now what can I do for you, young lady?"

Susan swallowed nervously.

"I—er—I want a job—not in Adelaide," she blurted. "At least—" she hesitated, and the man behind the desk smiled.

"How long have you been out here?" he asked. "You're from the Old Country, of course. What kind of job are you after—and where?"

"Well, I've been in Adelaide for two months," Susan told him, beginning to feel more at ease. "I came out under the Immigration Scheme and my sponsor is a friend of my family. I'm a shorthand-typist, and—well, that's what I was doing at home in Croydon, and now I'm working for Dalgetty's here in Adelaide." She stopped speaking, and the man behind the desk pulled a file towards him and flipped over some pages.

"Well—" he said at last, looking over his glasses at Susan, "I have quite a number of vacancies for typists and shorthand-typists, but what's wrong with the job you have? It's a good firm."

"Yes, I know," Susan agreed hastily. "It's just that—well, I really wanted something quite different —a different kind of job if possible, and not in Adelaide. Oh, I know, it's a nice town, I mean city, but—" she hesitated, and he finished dryly,

"Too much like Croydon, eh?"

Susan smiled with relief.

"Yes, that's just it," she said. "You see, what I want is to get out into the real Australia, not the towns. Towns are the same everywhere, don't you think? I want to see the Outback and the Great Barrier Reef, and the sugar plantations in Queensland, and the sheep stations, and——"

Mr Caldwell smiled broadly.

"A kind of walkabout job would suit you," he said, then added, "That's what the aborigines call it when they get 'itchy feet' and go off on the wander. However——" he pulled another file towards him, "What else can you do, besides shorthand-typing?" He looked across at her and Susan thought anxiously. Well, what else could she do that did not require specific qualifications?

"I——er——could housekeep," she ventured at last, rather anxiously. "I cooked and kept house for my father for four years and——er——" she came to a halt as she met the glance of the shrewd eyes across the desk.

"Bit young for that," he said. "What age are you, by the way?"

"Twenty——nearly twenty-one, and I——"

"Well, most of the housekeeping jobs I have, which incidentally are mainly in the Outback districts, are for older women, and the majority stipulate for widows——more experienced, perhaps," he added dryly.

"Oh!" sighed Susan, then she looked at him hopefully. "Aren't there just one or two who wouldn't mind——" but Mr Caldwell was busily looking through another file.

"Ever had anything to do with children?" he

asked suddenly. "Schools, part-time teaching, that sort of thing?"

Susan's face lit up. "Why, yes," she said. "I wanted to be a teacher, but I didn't do well enough at my G.C.E. But they took me on for nearly a year as a part-time teacher auxiliary. You see, there's a great shortage of teachers in England. I—I liked the job very much, but of course it came to an end when they got a qualified teacher; but I did like teaching." She paused, looked at Mr Caldwell, then added hopefully, "Is—is there any chance of getting a job in that line?"

"Ever heard of Australia's School of the Air? But of course you have," he said. "Now there's a job for you—right in the Interior—if that's really what you want."

Susan's eyes were bright with interest now, but suddenly they became clouded.

"Yes, of course I've heard of the School of the Air," she said. "But, as I just told you, I haven't any academic teaching qualifications, so—" but he interrupted her with a smile of encouragement.

"Never mind. You see, Miss Manley, for the jobs I have in mind that wouldn't matter. Practical experience in managing children is what's required, plus a readiness to make yourself useful in other ways."

"Oh, please tell me more!" Susan said eagerly. "As a matter of interest, I have a very good testimonial from the school where I taught as a part-timer. I could—"

"Yes, well—" he interrupted, "these jobs are for a kind of teacher-supervisor. The Headquarters of the School of the Air is here in Adelaide, and there are centres scattered throughout the country; one quite near here, as a matter of fact, at Port Augusta. They broadcast lessons to the children living on the cattle and sheep stations or any other isolated area. The pupils gather together in one place wherever there happens to be a transceiver, and—listen to their lessons coming to them over the air. Now—" Mr Caldwell grinned, "as you can imagine, these kids need supervising, or very little work would be done. In some places mothers have been doing the supervising jobs, but I gather it's not satisfactory; the kids play them up. You see, strict discipline must be maintained. Also most mums in these isolated districts are extremely busy women. So they've started employing partly-trained teachers to do the jobs, and I've heard that it's working very well, though the salaries are not much. Surprisingly enough, some of these supervisory teachers are fully trained and qualified and could earn far more at schools in the cities and towns." He smiled at Susan. "I can only assume that they like the jobs. However, for the most part, the teachers are people like yourself; just having practical experience of handling and instructing children." He paused and looked at Susan. "Well? Interested?"

"Oh, yes." Her voice was quite breathless. "It sounds—most interesting. What *is* the salary, Mr Caldwell?"

"About ten pounds a week—with your keep. Accommodation is usually arranged and paid for, with a family. Sometimes it's with the boss himself and his family; for it often happens that the children of the district whose fathers are mostly in his employ, meet in his house for the School of the Air sessions—

there's usually a room set apart. Now there's a correspondence school here in Adelaide which works in close conjunction with the School of the Air. If you are really interested and think you'd like to try your hand at the job, I'll give you the address and you can go along to Pennington Avenue and have a chat with the Principal. After that, and if you are *still* interested, come back here, and we'll have a look at the map and you can see just where there are jobs going—right?"

"Oh, thank you very much, Mr Caldwell." Susan's voice was slightly unsteady from the excitement that was bubbling up inside her. "I certainly *am* interested, and—" he handed her a paper on which he had written an address—"I'll go straightaway."

She hurried down the narrow staircase, then paused at the foot to study the address on the paper. Pennington Avenue. Yes, she knew exactly where that was—along King William Street, past the pleasant colourful public gardens and then on to the Cathedral. Tucking the paper into her handbag, she started off at a brisk pace and soon reached the Cathedral. She crossed the road over to the right, walked along a little way, and then, with quickly-beating heart, entered the building. Opposite her was a door marked 'Enquiries', and Susan knocked and walked in. At a table sat a pleasant-faced girl. She looked enquiringly at Susan.

"Could I—see the Principal, please?"

The girl picked up a telephone and spoke into it, and in a surprisingly short space of time Susan found herself facing the Principal of the Correspondence School, Adelaide.

"Yes, and what can I do for you?" he asked. "Do

sit down." Susan told him, and he listened to her with keen interest. He gave her a sheaf of pamphlets and talked to her about the various centres which broadcast to the outlying stations. "There's a School of the Air quite near here," he told Susan. "It's at Port Augusta, and caters for the children living in various parts of the Flinders range of mountains. Something like that might suit you, perhaps."

But she had other ideas. What she wanted was the real Outback which she knew was up towards the Northern Territory. The places she had read about before coming to Australia. Places like Darwin, Alice Springs, Cloncurry, and—but she was shy of mentioning them. She did not want to be thought just a silly little romantic. So Susan listened to this pleasant, helpful-sounding man, and then went back to see Mr Caldwell at the Employment Exchange.

That same evening, in their double room at the People's Palace, and as Pat was preparing for a date with Jack, Susan told of her visits to the Employment Bureau and the Education Centre at Pennington Avenue. As she came to the end of the recital of the day's activities, Pat turned from the dressing table and stared at her friend in consternation.

"Oh, Sue," she said at last, "I feel this is all my fault; but honestly, I never anticipated meeting Jack, and—"

"But that's all right," Susan interrupted her, laughing. "You needn't feel bad about it, Pat. We wouldn't have stayed together for ever, would we? I'm delighted about Jack, and of course it would have happened sooner or later anyway." She laughed again. "After all, it could have been me. But in any case, Pat, I don't want to stay in Adelaide; it just isn't my idea of Down-under." But Pat continued to look worried.

"No, well, it isn't mine either," she agreed. "And if it weren't for Jack, I'd have done the same. In fact, Sue, I half envy you, but—" a half smile wavered across her lips as she looked at Susan over her shoulder, "well, I really have fallen for Jack, and I *am* three years older than you, and I don't want to be left high and dry on the shelf."

"Why, of course," Susan said, smiling at her. "Though I can't imagine *you* on the shelf!"

"Oh, I don't know," Pat said, frowning. "The girls and fellows are getting married younger and younger these days—and I'm nearly twenty-four. But, Sue—" and here her face began to clear and she looked happier, "this is all terribly exciting. Are you sure you'll—"

"I'm not sure of anything," Susan interrupted, shaking her head and laughing again. She did a little jig round the room. "All I do know is that I'm dying to try it out!"

And that is how Susan Manley, late of Croydon, England, became teacher-supervisor at the cattle station of Kanoch Doon in North Queensland.

Mr Caldwell, at the Employment Bureau had advised her to think well over the whole business, especially that of going so far afield as North Queensland.

"There's a broadcasting station much nearer here," he had said more than once, "at Port Augusta. And we could probably fix you up at Wilpena Chalet where they have a transceiver set." But Susan had been quite firm in her decision to go up north, though

she was still shy of explaining why. It was the Outback of which she had read that she wanted to see,
the great interior of this vast country of Australia—
Alice Springs, Ayers Rock, the Devil's Marbles, and
the flat red plains round Tennant's Creek. She had
read of them and was now determined to see some
or all of them herself. Pat had also tried to persuade
her to take the job which was much closer at hand,
at Coober Pedy.

"Jack says it's quite near, but still out in the
desert," she said. "It's the opal mine place, where
Larry and Els came from, remember?"

Susan nodded. "Yes, I know," she said, and
grinned at Pat. "And from what they told us about
it, I don't think I'd want to stay there for long.
D'you know, Pat, the people there, gougers they're
called, live underground, in caves. Can you imagine
it?"

"Really!" Pat stared at her. "They never mentioned that; I suppose because they're so used to it.
In caves? Like the Ancient Britons?" She giggled. "I
wonder if they paint themselves with woad, and—
oh, Sue, I can just imagine you, dressed just in woad,
teaching the A.B.C. to your little pupils, also in—"
she rolled on her bed giggling again, and Susan joined
in. Then she said,

"Of course, I'd love to see it all, wouldn't you?
But from what Els told us of the flies and the heat,
and the dust, *and* the awful food—nearly everything
from tins—" She paused. "No, I guess Coober Pedy
can wait. What I want to see, and live among, are
the rolling downs, and the sheep, and the aborigine
stockmen, and the homesteads, and—"

"O.K., I get it, but I expect you'll get plenty of

heat, dust and flies up there too, though I admit it does sound more attractive. Jack says there are heaps of snakes, centipedes and huge lizards called goannas. Still want to go?" Susan laughed, and Pat went on, "You'll be fairly near to Alice Springs, won't you? I've always wanted to go there, after reading that book by Nevil Shute. Gosh, Sue, I expect the Outback will be full of stalwart, handsome sheep and cattle kings, all dying to settle down in their weatherboard palaces, with a nice little—"

"Well, I hope so," Susan interrupted, laughing, "eventually, anyway. You'd better get on with your dressing, Pat, or you'll have Jack knocking on the door any minute now."

CHAPTER 2

THEN began a period of intense excitement for Susan. She joyfully gave in her notice of departure to Dalgetty's, but not forgetting to thank them for all their kindness and help. Then she and Pat got out maps and leaflets and eagerly planned Susan's route to the cattle station of Kanoch Doon in North Queensland to which she had been assigned. She had been given two weeks before starting her job, as at present the children were on holiday. After much discussion, some argument with Jack and Pat, and many talks with the staff and guests at the Palace, Susan decided to travel by coach to Brisbane, capital of Queensland, then after a day's sightseeing, continue by coach along the Pacific Highway to Townsville where she planned to spend a couple of days.

"I shall be able to see the Great Barrier Reef from there," she told Pat, with shining eyes, "and Ted—" Ted was a sugar-cane cutter who was holidaying at the Palace—"says there's a marvellous undersea observatory at a place not far from Townsville. I must see that."

From Townsville Susan had been instructed to take an Ansett-Ana plane to a place in the interior called Shepton where she would be met by someone from Kanoch Doon cattle station.

"Gosh, if it weren't for Jack, how I'd love to be coming with you," Pat said enviously. "But there's one thing, Sue, I've made Jack promise that we'll go up that way for our honeymoon."

When the day of departure arrived, Pat, Jack and quite a number of friends Susan had made while staying at the Palace came to see her off. And as the big coach rumbled slowly out of the station Susan had her first moment of misgiving. Here she was, not yet twenty-one, all alone, and bound for a strange unknown country! Fortunately this mood did not last for long. 'What's the matter with you?' she asked herself impatiently. 'After all, if it doesn't work out you can always go back to Adelaide *and* probably get your old job back.' But in her heart Susan knew that she would never do that.

At Brisbane she spent a happy day sightseeing, then set off once more on the large comfortable coach for Townsville. Queer and fascinating names flashed past as they rolled along the excellent bitumen highway. Names like Prosperpine, Keppel Bay, Repulse Bay; all with an historical flavour. Eventually, after a night spent en route, the coach arrived at Townsville, a place of sunshine, gleaming white buildings and palm trees; and as Susan walked along the wide main street with its rows of palms running down the centre, and stared with wide eager eyes at the white-painted shops and cafés, she experienced for the first time since leaving England the real feel and smell of a foreign country. Peering up side streets, she could see into gardens full of orange and lemon trees, and with the flaming red of poinsettias and hibiscus. The very air seemed laden with the scent of the oranges and lemons.

Susan found that the under-sea observatory which Ted had told her about was situated at Green Island.

and that a local plane could get her there in quite a short time. She promptly decided to go. When she discovered that the island itself was a coral cay right on the reef itself her interest and excitement rose. First she visited the under-sea observatory, and after walking down some steps and into a large round compartment actually under the sea, felt she was in another world. She stood gazing with fascinated eyes at the beautiful formations of coral of all colours and shapes, and at the hundreds of fish, large and small and of every colour of the rainbow, weaving their tireless way between the convolutions of the coral.

Later that day she joined a party of tourists and the guide took them to see the Great Barrier Reef. He warned them before starting off to wear thick-soled shoes, as there were many dangerous kinds of marine life lurking in the pools, also the coral itself was a danger to bare feet. The Reef itself stretched for miles out to the open sea. It was low tide when they started and the sun was just beginning to sink towards the horizon. The reef was full of ridges and pools, and Susan stared down fascinated at the amazing world at her feet. Some of the pools were quite deep, and it seemed to her that wherever she looked there was something interesting and exciting to see. There were the shapes and patterns of the coral to begin with. There was a pale green mass which looked like a cluster of grapes, and jutting from an under-water shelf was something that looked like a miniature scarlet cactus plant. The guide pointed to a coral formation which looked like nothing so much as tiny hands with pink, purple and yellow fingers upheld in supplication and which he told them was called staghorn coral. 'And all this,' Susan thought with sudden awe, 'is the work of tiny polyps, and has been going on for millions of years. How tiny and insignificant it makes one feel!'

Moving among and in and out of the coral were marine shapes of every kind. There were darting fish of all shapes and colours, starfish, lobsters, crabs, molluscs and crustaceans. Susan's sharp eyes picked out something just under a rock which the guide told them was a slaver crab. It was squatting on a rock shelf just under the water, and seemed to be clutching something in each front claw.

"How does it get its name?" Susan enquired. "And what's that in its claws?"

"Well, I'll tell you. It's got an anemone in each claw. The crab prizes them from the rock. Then, as the poor trusting little blighter continues to fish with its tentacles, the crab, holding the anemone close to its mouth, extracts from it any morsel which takes his fancy, and pops it into his own mouth."

"Why, the greedy old so-and-so!" said one of the tourists. "Those poor little sea-anemones must wonder what happens to all the little tit-bits they catch!"

The next morning Susan returned to Townsville for the last leg of her journey to Kanoch Doon. She was looking forward with mixed feelings of pleasure and trepidation to starting her new job. The plane soon left the town behind, and then all Susan could see as she stared down was red sand, piles of enormous rocks and boulders, ranges of squat-looking hills, and occasional stretches of what she imagined to be mallee and spinifex. There seemed to be no buildings anywhere. It was not long before the plane began to circle above an air-strip surrounded by a few buildings, streets and green patches of grassland. This, she supposed, was Shepton, and as Susan stepped down on to the tarmac a man came striding towards her. He was tall and lean, and had something of the look of the sun-scorched background about him. He was wearing faded khaki trousers and a white shirt, and on his head was a wide-brimmed felt hat which shaded his face from the sun. He looked about twenty-eight, Susan thought, and his teeth shone very white as he smiled at her and held out a hand.

"Hello," he said, holding Susan's hand in a firm grip. "You'll be Miss Susan Manley, I guess. My name's Ian McQuarrie, from Kanoch Doon Homestead." He released her hand and looked about him. "Have you much baggage with you?" Susan indicated her two suitcases and returned his friendly smile, at the same time noticing the intense blueness of his eyes. "Right," he said, as he picked up the cases. "Over here, Miss Manley, I've got the ute waiting."

Susan followed him out on to a deserted bitumen road which seemed to lead to nowhere. He stowed the cases in the back, then helped Susan into the vehicle. "Reckon you're pretty tired, Miss Manley," he observed, "but we'll be at the Homestead in a couple of hours."

"No, I'm not the least tired," Susan assured him. "I broke my journey at Townsville; I did so want to see the Great Barrier Reef."

He nodded. "And what did you think of it?"

"Oh, I just haven't words to describe it," Susan told him. "It was far, far more wonderful than I imagined."

He nodded again, then turned to smile at her.

"Folks round here will be damned glad to see you,"

he said. "Kids have been running wild for—well, it seems like months to their mothers, I guess, but it's really only a matter of weeks. Kate Dunhill, one of the mothers, ran the school for a couple of months, but she had to give it up; too many other chores to do."

"How many children are there?" Susan asked, looking out of the car at the endlessly stretching plains and the brazen sky above. In the far distance were curiously flat-topped mountains; not very lofty and of a dull reddish colour. There was nothing in between but burnt-looking earth with just an occasional clump of bare twisted trees.

"About ten, I guess. You'll find them very shy at first, but when they get used to you—" he smiled, "and have got you weighed up, well—!" he grinned again. "But you'll be able to manage them, they're just ordinary lively kids, that's all."

Susan took another glance around her. The harsh plain with its twisted skeletons of trees had given place to patchy brown and green stretches of land with an occasional fence which seemed to lead off into nowhere. Almost imperceptibly the land became greener, with patches of really green grass with some cattle grazing on it. She saw a tall structure with a kind of wheel at the top which her companion told her was an artesian well. Then, in the distance, and gleaming white under the brassy sky, Susan had her first glimpse of Kanoch Doon Homestead. It stood out starkly like a pale cut-out pasted on to its background. Compared with the immensity all around, it looked ridiculously small, but grew rapidly larger as the utility put on speed. Quite soon it became a large white-painted weatherboard bungalow with railings of delicate black iron tracery outlining its broad verandas. Wide curved wooden steps ran up to the centre of the front veranda, and a bright yellow creeper which Susan thought she recognised as cassia spread up and over the veranda pillars. The wide wooden shutters at the open windows were painted a gay pink. At one side of the house were two huge tanks, round and silvery in the glare of the sun, and next to each of them was a concrete and brick structure which Susan took to be the shower houses. Surrounding the house were spacious lawns and flower beds, and she stared in amazement at the fresh green of the grass, and the bright colours of the shrubs and flowers. Ian McQuarrie pointed and then turned to Susan.

"Well, there you are," he said. "There's the homestead of Kanoch Doon; been there for well over a hundred years, though I guess that doesn't seem very long to you. The house has been built on to, of course. It started as not much more than a shack, built by my great-grandfather, and called after his ancestral home in the highlands of Scotland."

Susan could hear the pride in his voice and thought she could understand it.

"It's beautiful," she said. "You must feel very attached to it, Mr McQuarrie. Have you lived here always?"

He nodded. "Yes, all my life. Rooms and outhouses have been added from time to time; verandas and lawns and gardens, till," he smiled down into her animated face, "you see it as it is to-day—Kanoch Doon Homestead and cattle station. Apart from the manager's house, the store-keeper's place, and the stockmen's quarters, the next homestead is nearly a hundred miles away with another about the same distance in the opposite direction—those two are our nearest neighbours. Some of your pupils come from them." He waved to someone on the veranda. "Well, here we are. Welcome to Kanoch Doon, Miss Manley."

The utility turned in at a wide gate, then up a long dusty drive which led directly to the house. As they drew up before the flight of wide steps Susan looked up in some apprehension, for the wide veranda seemed to be full of people; but a slightly-built elderly woman with a pale gentle face came forward at once to greet her.

"Welcome to Kanoch Doon," she called in a clear pleasant voice. "You'll be Miss Susan Manley, of course. Come along in." She came down the steps as Ian helped Susan out of the car. "I'm Helen McQuarrie, or Auntie Mac to most." She took Susan's hand in hers and shook it. "Now come and meet the others."

Susan followed her on to the veranda where two young men hastily got to their feet. They were both as tall as Ian. Behind them was a young girl. "This is Milton, our jackeroo," Mrs McQuarrie continued, "and this is Denis, a neighbour." The two young men lunged awkwardly forward and engulfed Susan's hand, one after the other, in hard brown fists. They smiled shyly at her. "Now where's Melissa gone?" Mrs McQuarrie looked round and beyond the young man. "And Letty? She was here a minute ago."

"They're making tea, I guess, Auntie Mac," Denis, the older of the two put in. "Here they are." Two girls in checked shirts and faded denims appeared at the door leading into the house. One was fair, with large pale blue eyes, and the other, a few years younger, was a plump redhead. They carried laden trays which they placed on a side table.

"Come on over here and met Miss Susan Manley," Mrs McQuarrie called to them; and as the girls approached she took the arm of the redhead. "This is my daughter Melissa," she said to Susan, "and this—" she nodded in the direction of the other girl, "is Letty French, a neighbour."

The tall fair girl smiled in a rather appraising fashion, Susan thought as they shook hands, but Melissa, the younger girl, grinned and said,

"Hiya," then added, "Do we have to call you Miss Manley?"

"Of course not. Susan's my name." She saw that Ian had reappeared after putting the car away. He smiled at her as he came up the veranda steps.

"Where's that tea, Ma?" he called. "I bet Miss Manley could do with a cup, and so could I !"

"Well, sit down, everyone," his mother said placidly. "Melissa, you carry the cups and plates round."

Susan sat down in a comfortable cane chair and Ian sat beside her with Denis on the other side. As she drank her tea she looked about her with interest. Melissa, the young daughter—she looked about seventeen, Susan thought—was chattering away to Milton, the jackeroo, while Letty French, the other girl, was talking to Mrs McQuarrie. Then, as she watched, someone else appeared at the door leading into the house, an elderly man, tall and with thick greying hair. The father, Susan thought, and at the same moment she heard her hostess say,

"Come over here and meet the new teacher, Dad."
Susan smiled and stood up as he approached.

"Welcome, my dear," he said, holding out a hand.
"My, but you're just a bairn! I hope you'll be happy
with us."

"I'm sure I shall, Mr McQuarrie," Susan murmured shyly, then as he moved away she resumed
her seat beside Denis. Ian had joined his father and
they were talking in low tones by the door. She
looked out again over the wide paddocks, and beyond
them to the flat plain and the low foothills. A feeling
of peace and content swept over her, and she knew
she was to find happiness in this place.

"You're from England, of course." It was Denis
speaking, and he was looking into Susan's heart-
shaped face with the large black-lashed grey-green
eyes with obvious appreciation. She nodded, and he
added with a smile, "Well, it's nice to have you here.
You were in Adelaide for a short time, I believe.
Didn't you like city life?"

"Well—" she hesitated, "I wanted a real change.
Life in Adelaide was too much like life in England.
It wasn't what I'd been looking for."

"And that was—?" It was Ian's voice, and Susan
looked up at him as he spoke. He was smiling down
at her. She hesitated again, then laughed a trifle self-
consciously.

"I—don't know, of course," she said at last. "Who
does? But—" she looked up and returned his smile,
"the looking is great fun, anyway!"

"Well, I hope you find it here," he said half-
jokingly, and at the same moment Letty French's
rather penetrating voice came from the other side of
the veranda.

"And how's Alan these days?" she asked. "I don't seem to have seen him in months." There was a sudden silence on the veranda and then Mrs McQuarrie murmured something which Susan could not hear. She glanced up again at Ian and saw that he was now staring in front of him. Mr McQuarrie made a sudden movement towards the door, and then all at once everyone seemed to be talking again. Susan felt puzzled, and wondered if she had imagined each person seemed to be waiting for the other to speak first.

Soon after this Denis rose to go and Mrs McQuarrie suggested to Melissa that she should take Susan to see her room. It was at the side of the house, along a covered way which led off from the veranda, and was a little apart from the rest of the house. The room itself was large and airy and comfortably furnished as a bed-sitting room.

"Like it?" Melissa asked. "Mum thought you'd prefer a room where you could sit and read sometimes, or mark the kids' books, and—well, be on your own if you felt like it."

"I think it's lovely, Melissa," said Susan, standing and looking about her. "I'm glad I came here, I'm sure I'm going to love it all."

The other girl smiled. "I'm glad you've come, too," she said. "Well, come up to the house if you feel like it, but if not, breakfast's at eight. 'Bye for now."

Susan did not return to the house that night. Instead she unpacked, then went early to bed. But not to sleep, unfortunately. For the interest and excitement of her journey from Adelaide to Townsville, the visit to the Great Barrier Reef, and then at last the meeting with the McQuarrie family had so over-stimulated her that she had lain wide-eyed in her comfortable bed, hour after hour, just listening to the unaccustomed night sounds, and thinking of this family with whom she would be living. She liked Ian, the quiet-voiced son of the house; Mrs McQuarrie was quite sweet, Susan decided, and the father too, though a man of few words, looked nice and dependable. Of the two girls, Susan liked Melissa, the daughter, but was not so sure of the older girl, Letty French. Who was Alan? she suddenly wondered. No one had replied to Letty's question and it seemed to have rather upset Mr McQuarrie, who had risen soon after and gone into the house. She had slept at last with the question still in her mind, and awakened suddenly to a golden dawn.

'I'm here, in North Queensland,' Susan thought, and at once jumped from her bed and went to the window for a glimpse of the unfamiliar scene. The rising sun was just behind the rampart of ochre-coloured hills on the horizon. The sky all round was suffused with delicate swathes of pink and apricot; and even as Susan watched with half-held breath a tiny sliver of gold appeared on the topmost ridge; and then, it seemed almost immediately, the round golden ball swam up above the hills and the entire plain was steeped in its golden light. Susan's eyes ranged delightedly over the scene spread out before her, and then her breath was released in a big sigh. The wide paddocks stretched to right and left, brown with patches of green and broken up at intervals by clumps of trees and shrubs. Beyond this was the plain, just yellowish earth with a few stunted skeletons of trees dotted about. And beyond this was the range of red blunt-topped hills looking rather like castle ramparts. 'Yes, this is the Australia I wanted to see,' Susan thought; the land of the wide open spaces, the land of the Never-Never; the land of the mysterious aborigines who had their homes, when they had homes at all in the caves of these solid-looking hills. Yes, this is what she had longed to see. Not the cities with their hotels and shops, and tidy parks and recreation grounds.

Regretfully she turned away from the entrancing view at her window and started to dress. This was her first morning with her pupils and she wanted to be in good time for them. Nervousness was beginning to overcome her. 'After all,' she thought, 'this is an entirely new venture, not like the one at home where I was supervised all the time by qualified teachers. This is going to be up to me and no one else!'

Quickly she finished her dressing, stepped outside on to the covered way and walked along the veranda to the main building. There seemed to be no one about, but from some nearby gum trees came the sound of birdsong. Though she had been in Australia but a short time Susan recognised the bellbird and thought it sounded very sweet and pure here in the silence of the plains. She sniffed appreciatively. There was a freshness, an unused quality in the air—so different from the stale air of the towns and cities, Susan thought. Then to her nostrils was wafted another smell. It came from inside the house and was compounded of frying steak, grilled bacon, and toast. Mrs McQuarrie appeared at the open door

"Ah, there you are, my dear," she said in her clear yet soft voice. "You must be ready for your breakfast. The boys and Melissa will be in any minute now.

Come and sit down. What will you have to eat? There's steak and eggs, egg and bacon, kidneys—did you sleep well?"

Susan laughed. "Hello," she said, then added, "No, not very well. I think I was too excited. I'll have egg and bacon, please." As she took a chair at the table Ian came in, closely followed by Milton and Melissa.

"Good morning," they said to her almost in chorus, then with a scraping of chairs everyone sat down. Mr McQuarrie now appeared at the door. He nodded and smiled at Susan, then took his place at the head of the table. The chattering subsided as he took one swift glance around, then bowed his head.

"For what we are about to receive may the Lord make us truly thankful," he said quietly, then raised his head and took a long thirsty drink of tea from the cup which his wife had just handed to him.

'Even the egg and bacon tastes different,' Susan thought, attacking the generously piled-up plate which Mrs McQuarrie had put before her.

"Those dingoes had a busy night," Ian remarked to his father as he reached for the bottle of sauce.

"Oh, what?" Mr McQuarrie put down his cup and waited.

"Tried to get through the fence in several places, but I've fixed it. It's O.K. now."

"What about the cattle?"

"All right," Ian said laconically, then he looked across the table at Susan. A smile creased his lean handsome face. "Ready for those kids?" he asked. "The young Bronsons are here already. Their dad works for us and they have a small homestead only a couple of miles away, so they haven't far to come. The others are some distance away; the Willcocks' kids nearly a hundred miles; they come in their dad's plane—a Cessna. You'll hear it touching down any minute now."

Susan gave a sudden laugh and the others looked up at her enquiringly.

"I was just thinking," she said rather shyly. "The contrast, you know. The kiddies at home who come to school in the school bus, or walk from just round the corner of the street, and here, coming to school every morning in an aeroplane. It's the strangeness of it all."

As Susan finished speaking she heard the plane, very faintly at first, then getting louder and louder, and then the final and intermittent phut-phut as the machine grounded. Then—silence.

Ian smiled at her again. "That'll be the lot," he remarked. The meal was soon over as everyone concentrated on eating, then Ian rose and looked at Susan. "I'll take you over and introduce you to your pupils," he said as chairs were pushed back and there was a general move.

Mrs McQuarrie and Melissa started busily to clear the table as Mr McQuarrie lighted his pipe, then disappeared into the back regions. Susan followed Ian on to the front veranda. The freshness of early morning had given way to a still heat which she knew would increase as the day wore on. There were many signs of life now about the homestead and its surroundings. She could see spirals of smoke rising from several buildings which she supposed were the men's quarters. In the near-distance she could see khaki-clad men on horses in and around the paddocks, and to the left of her were several tractors and pieces of farm machinery. There were also dogs, mostly of the collie or sheep dog type. One advanced hesitatingly to Susan and sniffed round her ankles, then with lolling tongue and slowly-waving tail he reached to lick her hand.

"Hello, Rags," said Ian, aiming a playful kick at the animal. "You're honoured, Susan. Rags doesn't take to everyone, very choosy dog he is." He looked down into her face. "Er—d'you mind if I call you Susan?"

"Of course not." She followed him across the side lawn towards a concrete structure which was joined to the main bulding by a roofed passage.

"Well, here we are," Ian said, "your schoolroom." He unlocked the door and stood aside for Susan to enter. She looked about her. It was a pleasant room with venetian blinds at the windows. There were about a dozen small desks with chairs. At the far end was a larger desk with a chair behind it, and at the other was the plain insignificant transceiver set. Yes, plain and ordinary-looking, Susan thought, but it was the means by which the children of the lonely Outback were in touch with learning, culture, and, most important of all, other children from all over the vast continent. And they had John Flynn and Adelaide Mietke to thank for it, she thought, for Susan had recently been reading the story of John Flynn and the Flying Doctor Service which had started with the pedal radio. From that had been developed this modern transceiver which yet was so simple that a child of six could understand and use it. Susan had also read the story of how Miss Mietke, on a visit to one of the R.F.D.S. bases, had seen the possibilities of these transceivers in connection with the children of the isolated districts. She had approached the

R.F.D.S. H.Q., and eventually her suggestions had been adopted.

Susan suddenly saw that Ian was watching her with a slightly puzzled smile on his face.

"Well," he said, "you were far away then. What were you thinking?"

"I was thinking of this job of mine, and how it all started. John Flynn and the flying doctors, and also Miss Adelaide Mietke, you know, and—what a wonderful thing it is."

He nodded, his eyes taking in the flush of enthusiasm in her cheeks and the light in her eyes.

"Yes, it's certainly made all the difference to the kids," he agreed. He followed her further into the room and nodded to the transceiver. "D'you understand these things?"

Susan nodded eagerly. "Yes, they showed me at the Education Centre at Adelaide," she said. "Is there anything on now?"

Ian looked at his watch. "No, it's still the flying doctor service. The schools' broadcast started at nine-forty-five and carries on till eleven. It starts off again at something past two and finishes around four. I have a time-table for you."

Susan was looking thoughtful. "There's a big gap between the morning and afternoon session," she said. "Surely the children don't go back to their homes for lunch."

"No." He shook his head. "They stay here and my mother, Auntie Mac as they all call her, gives them lunch. Then I believe the other teacher used to go over the morning lessons after the kids had had a bit of a rest." He paused for a moment, then looked smilingly into her slightly anxious face. "Well, are you ready to tackle them? They're all waiting to meet the new teacher; can you hear them?"

Susan *had* heard the scuffling and muted voices for some time; and now, as she and Ian left the school-room and stepped back on to the veranda, she saw them, grouped together and trying hard not to stare at her. Ian called to them, and they advanced a few paces.

"Come and meet Miss Manley, your new teacher," he said. And one by one the dozen or so children came awkwardly forward and shook hands. "Well," said Ian, turning to Susan, "I guess I must leave you now. Got all the keys? Nothing else you want?" He smiled down at her, showing his strong white teeth, then touched the brim of his shabby old hat and strode off in the direction of the stables.

Susan looked at the group of boys and girls who stood there and stared back at her. They were of all ages from about six to twelve or thirteen, and as she gazed back at them she felt horribly uncertain of herself and her capabilities.

"Er—shall we go in?" she said, and with one accord they trooped eagerly after her and into the classroom. "Sit down," she added, turning to face them. "Well, first I must know your names, so I'll call the register." She saw that the book had been placed ready for her on the desk. "Now, will you step forward as I call your name? Right."

The register was duly called, and Susan began to feel more confident as she turned to consult the time-table which had been given to her in Adelaide at the Correspondence School. The children looked at her silently, then the biggest boy, whose name was Martin, spoke up.

"We always git round the radio for assembly and prayers," he said. Susan glanced at her watch. She saw that it was just nine-forty-five and time for the school of the air to start. A little tremor of excitement made her catch her breath.

"Right," she said, "gather round, then."

"Can I throw the switch, Miss?" Mary, a small girl of about eight, asked her eagerly. "Mrs Dunhill always let us."

Susan nodded and joined the circle of children. The first lesson on the time table was reading for grade one, and as she sat down, Mary threw the switch across the face of the transceiver. There was a short pause, then a voice came through, clear and strong.

"This is VDM 2, R.F.D.S. Medical station. The time is now nine-forty-five. We are ready for the morning School of the Air." There was another short pause, then came the sound of piano music playing a lively tune.

"That's the signature tune, Miss," Martin informed Susan with an air of importance. The group of children straightened up and waited expectantly. The music stopped and the teacher's voice, a woman's, came across to them from far-away Alice Springs.

"Hello there," she said. "Good morning, children. Now, let's hear who is listening. Over to you!" Roll-call had begun, and presently Susan heard their own call-sign XXV 3, and the children with her here in the schoolroom each answered to their names. All the code signals used by the two-way transceivers in homesteads, Mission stations and outcamps on the Flying Doctor Radio Network were called out and answers received. Susan sat entranced and listened to it all.

"Are you listening?" came the teacher's voice once more. "We will now have our morning hymn. Ready?"

Susan's small class shot to their feet as the familiar strains of 'All things bright and beautiful' came through. At first the children seemed shy of singing in front of this stranger, but as Susan herself joined in heartily, they began to lose their shyness. Then to Susan's surprise, the voice of the teacher said, "We would like to give a welcome to Miss Susan Manley at Kanoch Doon station, who has just joined the School of the Air." It was so unexpected that Susan felt herself blushing furiously. The children stared at her with lively curiosity.

"That's you, isn't it, Miss?" said Mary; and as Susan nodded and smiled, her imagination was busily at work. She could almost see the other woman in the small empty room at Alice Springs sitting behind her desk; the piano not far away, the transceiver in front of her—and her pupils scattered far and wide, over hill and plain, but all in touch and bound to her for a short time by a common interest.

The teacher's voice came again and Susan wrenched her thoughts back to the present. The English lesson had started. Grades two and three were given passages to read silently, while Grade One listened to the teaching. Susan's watchful eyes at once saw that the children of grades two and three, two small boys and a little girl of the same age, seemed to regard this as a suitable time to idle. They whispered and giggled at each other, and the bigger boy produced a toy boomerang from his pocket.

"James, put that away," ordered Susan, "or shall I?" The toy promptly disappeared as James gave her a reproachful look. "Now," she went on, "you three children come over to the other side of the room, and I'll hear you read in turn."

"Mrs Dunhill used to let us draw pictures from our books," the small girl said, looking hopefully at Susan.

"Well, I might do that—after I've heard you read."

Jane smiled at Susan and opened her book, which Susan saw with pleased surprise was a 'Janet and John,' a series with which she was quite familiar. As she listened to the reading half Susan's attention was directed to the six older children in Grade One.

"Martin Gregson," she heard the far-away teacher say, "your essay on 'Creatures of the Desert' was very good, but you must be careful of the punctuation. There is a difference between a full stop and a semi-colon. Here is an example"—So the lesson went on; and as Susan watched and listened she saw why the previous teacher had set the three younger children to draw when they would not require much supervision; for Grade One was not paying the attention to the lesson it should, and she could see how very necessary was the teacher-supervisor. So quickly Susan switched the three younger children to doing some copy-writing while she herself moved over to superintend the senior class. The older children looked knowingly at each other, but after a firm but decisive word from Susan the inconsequent chatter stopped and they gave their attention to the unseen teacher.

"Now, Josephine, from XXV 3," came the clear voice, "I believe you had an arithmetic problem last Friday which you couldn't solve. Well, to-morrow I shall be dealing with it, so don't forget to bring your book with you. We will now pass on to the next lesson, which is geography. Open your atlases at page forty-five. I hope you have them all ready." Susan gave a swift glance round during the pause that followed and saw that all the books were indeed open and at the ready. This was evidently a popular lesson, and while it was going on she was able to conduct a simple number lesson with Grade Three.

The conclusion of the geography lesson brought them to the end of the morning session. Susan dismissed her small flock, who promptly disappeared in the direction of the kitchen. She did a bit of tidying up, then followed them and found Mrs McQuarrie, or Auntie Mac as the children called her, busily dispensing lunch at the big kitchen table. She gave Susan a generously piled-up plate, and smiled brightly at her. "All right?" her raised eyebrows seemed to ask, and Susan nodded.

After the children had had their meal they sat or played on the roomy back veranda while the rest of the household had theirs. The meal finished, as did almost all meals in Australia, with a large pot of tea. Susan then assembled her small flock and told them firmly to take a rest in the long cane lounge chairs put out for their particular use. Two of the boys had wandered off to the paddocks, but Ian told Susan not to worry.

"I'll chase them back," he told her; and Susan and the rest of the children had barely settled down before the two boys, Martin and James, arrived back, looking breathless and excited.

"There's a willie-willie coming up," they told Susan, and Martin asked, "Ever seen one, Miss?" She shook her head, and he urged hopefully, "Well, come and have a look."

Susan glanced at her watch hesitantly.

"Come on, Miss," urged Martin. "It's early; school don't start for another five minutes, I saw the time in the store." She saw that he was right, so without wasting any more time followed the prancing children out on to the veranda. Martin pointed, and Susan saw what looked exactly like a whirlpool, but in sand. It swept up abruptly from the ground, stretched itself into an elongated funnel, then opened out and thinned away into the shimmering heat haze. It moved rapidly along the ground; and whizzing circles of sand and rubble with small tufts of trees and shrubs were left in its wake. It was some distance away, but Susan was sure that she could smell its dusty breathlessness.

"It's goin' away," Martin said regretfully, then looked at Susan in a slightly superior fashion. "It's caused by the heat—and the extremes," he said. "Yer see, the hot air drags it up, and because the sand's all loose, it rushes in with the cold stream, see?" Susan smiled and nodded into the bright intelligent eyes which were raised to hers. "I know," he went on, "because I wrote and asked the teacher at the Alice. Now you've come and I can ask you questions, can't I?"

"Yes, of course, Martin," Susan said, "though I might not have been able to answer that one. But if there's anything else you want to know—" she paused. "And if I didn't know, I could always find out. So do ask by all means."

"Still, I 'spect you know a good bit," Martin conceded generously as they all trooped back to the classroom.

The afternoon timetable listed spelling; and again the teacher's voice from far-away Alice Springs came through to them. A spelling competition started, and Susan was pleased to see the eager interest shown by her own pupils.

"That's very good, Martin Gregson from XXV 3," came the clear voice, and Susan had to hide a smile as she saw the way the boy preened himself before her and the other children.

The School of the Air session ended for the day at three-forty-five. Susan then read them a story which lasted till four o'clock, and so ended the first day at her new job. As the children filed out of the classroom Mary Reid, the eldest girl, turned to her and said shyly,

"I'm glad you've come to Kangaroo, Miss."

Susan stared at her in surprise. "Well, thank you, Mary," she said, "but I don't quite understand. What, or where, is Kangaroo?"

Mary looked puzzled, but Martin Gregson cut in with a grin.

"Oh, it's what the abos call the McQuarrie Homestead, and now nearly everyone calls it that. I don't think the abos can say Kanoch Doon, and it sounds like Kangaroo to them. See? Can we have some home work, Miss?" Susan laughed. She was still thinking of Kangaroo and the abos. "Can we?"

"Homework? Why, yes, of course," she said. "How about writing the story I've just read, in your own words?"

Mary looked dubious. "Oh, I dunno 'bout that," she said, but Martin cut in with a confident,

"That's easy. O.K., Ma'am."

"Oh, listen, children!" Susan called, and the

children stopped their preparations for departure and looked at her expectantly. "My name is Susan Manley," she said. "And I don't much like being called 'Miss' or 'Ma'am'. Can you think of something nicer, more friendly?"

Martin giggled and whispered something to James, who giggled back but shook his head. After a short pause Mary said shyly and awkwardly,

"How 'bout Miss Susan?"

"That suits me fine. Come on, Rob, I want to see this Cessna plane of yours."

"Well, well," Mrs McQuarrie said to Susan about ten minutes later as she mounted the steps of the veranda, "and how did the first day go off?"

"Quite well, I think," Susan said, showing her nice white even teeth in a bright smile. "They're a nice bunch of kids, and everything was fine."

"Good. Well now, you'd like a shower, I'm sure. Tea's at six."

After the meal which at home in Croydon Susan would have called supper everyone trooped out on to the pleasant front veranda and proceeded to relax after the day's work. The men had changed into clean white shirts, and Susan thought what a handsome pair of men were Ian and his father, Douglas McQuarrie. She caught the eye of the former as she thought this and knew that she was blushing. Melissa brought out the inevitable large pot of tea, but there was also a pot of coffee. A cool breeze was blowing across the wide paddocks and the plains beyond and the entire landscape was flooded with golden sunset light.

"Tea or coffee, Susan?" Melissa asked. "Tea for you, Dad?" Susan asked for coffee and Melissa began to rattle cups and saucers.

"Do you ride, Susan?" Ian suddenly asked. He smiled at her.

"Well—" she hesitated for a moment. "Yes, I used to ride as a child when we lived in the country, but that's some years ago, I'm afraid."

"Well, how about an early ride to-morrow? We've got a nice quiet old mare who'd suit you fine—to begin with?"

"Yes, I'd love it," Susan agreed eagerly.

"Right. About six suit you? Not too early?" She shook her head vigorously, and then the talk became general. Susan found that her heart was beating at rather more than its usual rate, and she was filled with a pleasant sense of anticipation. Melissa started to pass cups round; Ian and his father began a low-voiced discussion on some farming matter, and then suddenly looked up as the clatter of horse's hooves was heard in the distance.

"I bet that's Letty," said Melissa, and glanced across at her brother. "Yes, here she comes." Susan looked out and saw the cantering roan with the girl rider approaching in a cloud of dust.

"Hi!" Letty French called, and waved her riding whip. Ian rose and went to grasp the horse's reins as the girl dismounted. "Thought I'd ride over and remind you about the barbecue at Anderson's place. You're all coming, aren't you? It's tomorrow."

"Well, I don't know," said Ian, starting to lead the horse away. "I'd forgotten all about it, as a matter of fact."

"I expect Susan would like to go," Mrs McQuarrie put in. "Hello, Letty, staying for a while?"

"I'd like to stay overnight if it's O.K. with you, Auntie Mac."

"Why, yes, of course." But Susan thought that Mrs McQuarrie did not sound too enthusiastic. Ian returned at that moment and followed Letty up the steps to the veranda.

"You'll be able to go riding with Ian and Susan in the morning," said Melissa. "That's if you can drag yourself up at six a.m."

Susan smiled across at Letty, but then thought she detected a sudden tightening of the other girl's lips, and began to wonder about her—and Ian. Was there anything between these two? And was Letty beginning to get jealous? Susan hoped not. Life was so full of interest and excitement just now that she did not want any complications of this kind to spoil it.

"Oh, here's a letter for you, Auntie Mac," said Letty, seating herself beside Ian. "It was put in our box by mistake." She dived a hand into the pocket of her riding jacket and passed it across.

Mrs McQuarrie looked at the address, then slipped the letter into the pocket of her dress. Douglas McQuarrie looked at his wife, who nodded briefly. Susan saw that Ian and Milton, the jackeroo, had also glanced quickly at Mrs McQuarrie, then away again. There was a sudden silence, short and almost unnoticeable, and she had the slightly uneasy feeling that perhaps the letter would have been opened and read if she had not been there. Was it from the mysterious Alan? she wondered. Conversation started up again. Susan had a second cup of coffee, then rose and said her goodnights to the others. Though it was still quite early she wanted to be alone in her own room to quietly savour the events of the day, then perhaps write a letter to Pat in Adelaide.

After undressing and getting into a housecoat,

Susan stood at the open window of her bed-sitting room and looked out at the starlit night. It was almost as bright as day; and beyond the dusty track leading from the homestead to the outer gates she could see faintly the bitumen road stretching out bare and flat right out to where it merged into the deep shadow of the foothills. It was all very quiet, the only sound being the faint and intermittent murmur of the voices from the front veranda. Soon these also ceased and she could just hear the indistinguishable and far-off sound of the wild creatures in the hills.

'It's lovely here,' Susan thought, leaning far out of the window to catch the faint breeze, 'one can almost hear the silence.' She drew in a deep breath of the pure cool air, then let it out on a long sigh of contentment. 'There's a feeling of freedom. I'm going to love it here, I know. I like the job, and I like the people—and that's enough to go on with.' But as she got into bed her thoughts turned to Ian McQuarrie, the son of the house, and she found herself wishing that Letty French were not coming riding with them. 'I would like to get to know Ian,' she thought, and 'to-morrow would have been a wonderful beginning.' Beginning to what? her thoughts seemed to ask, but she shrugged her shoulders impatiently, and got out her writing pad. She wrote a long and enthusiastic letter to Pat, put out the light and was asleep almost before her head had touched the pillow.

She was awakened at six by a shout from outside her window. It was Ian and there was no sign of Letty. But even as Susan ran down the steps to join Ian, the other girl appeared at the door hastily buttoning up her jacket. Susan was conscious of a feeling of disappointment, but soon forgot it in the excitement and exhilaration of the ride. The air was like wine, the horse Ian had had saddled for her was quiet and well-trained, but not too much so. Susan's first nervousness soon wore off, and when the other two horses broke into a brisk canter, and hers followed suit as is the way of horses, she quickly reacted to the exhilarating exercise and felt like laughing aloud for sheer joy of life. They rode out towards the distant range of hills which Ian told Susan was part of the lower slopes of the Great Dividing Range. In less than half an hour they reached a deep gully, and there Susan made the acquaintance of two aborigine stockmen, the first she had seen. They nodded and smiled at her with their broad flat features, and indicated the blackened billycan which one of them was swinging from side to side, and then right over his head.

"This is the first of the mustering camps," Ian told Susan as he helped her to dismount. "There are twelve in all at further and further distances from the cattle station. When the cattle are all mustered, or rounded up, they're driven down to the station to be sorted out ready for the trucks to take them to market."

"Tea ready, Boss Ian!" one of the stockmen called.

"Ever had billy tea, Susan?" Ian asked, then as she shook her head, "Then you've missed something real bonzer. O.K.," he called, and nodded to the boys, who produced some tin mugs. Ian watched as they rinsed them thoroughly in hot water before adding the milk.

"Umm, good," Susan smiled a few seconds later as she took her first sip of the steaming liquid. "But tell me, why was he swinging the billy? Right over his head, too."

The others laughed, and Letty said,

"It's supposed to improve the flavour, and it draws quickly. It really does seem to make a difference."

"There's a pool a little lower down the gully," said Ian, "and after the wet there's enough water for swimming."

"I love swimming," said Susan, "and it's not too far to come either."

"I wouldn't come alone," Ian said quickly. "You see, one can soon get out of sight of the homesteads and paddocks. The country looks flat, but really it undulates, and if a willy-willy starts up suddenly the lie of the land can change completely; there could be hills where none were before, familiar trees and bushes could be uprooted so that landmarks disappear and everything looks different. So—" he grinned at her and shook his head. "See what I mean?" Susan smiled and nodded, and Ian looked at his watch.

"Time to be starting back," he said. "We've all got a day's work ahead of us. How are you liking yours, Susan?"

"I love it; in fact I'm loving everything at present."

Letty looked at her. "It's early days, of course," she remarked as the three of them remounted the horses and started back for Kanoch Doon.

School went well that morning. The principal subject was number work which seemed to hold the interest of most of the children. Susan passed among them giving a word of advice here and there; and sometimes finding it necessary to give a word of admonishment when the replies through the transceiver to the unseen teacher at Alice Springs became too loud and eager. She was intrigued to note that all the problems and examples given to the children were couched in terms familiar to these country children, such as the varying speeds of tractors, horses, cattle and cattle trains, and many others. Fractions and weights and measures were of commodities they were likely to see and handle in the general stores attached to the homesteads and small stations. The morning seemed to fly by, and then it was time for the children's dinner.

"Auntie Mac," Martin Gregson said as the children sat round the big kitchen table enjoying a salad meal, "how big's this room?"

"I've no idea, son."

"Shall I measure it for you? Might come in useful to know. I could tell you the area of this kitchen." He looked at her with bright, eager eyes.

"Well, yes, you could, but finish your dinner first, dear."

"O.K., but it *is* measuring work this afternoon, isn't it, Miss Susan, and we ought to get in some practice." He nodded to the other children and the meal was finished in record time. The afternoon was spent by the older children in darting busily from veranda to schoolroom, thence to the bathrooms, and finishing up with measuring the tables, chairs and cupboards of the entire house. While this was going on the three small ones drew pictures and read from the 'Janet and John' reading books, and chatted happily to Susan and each other. Susan apologised afterwards to Mrs McQuarrie for the invasion of the house, but the latter just laughed indulgently.

"Don't worry about that," she said. "The kids were happy and busy, and learning something useful, and I like to hear their chatter anyway."

Letty French had departed homeward earlier in the day after reminding Ian again about the barbecue. Susan had been looking forward to this event, but something intervened—something which put all thoughts of barbecues out of everyone's head. Susan was about to dismiss her small school when Martin suddenly raised his head from a box which he was carefully measuring and said,

"Hi, kin you smell burning?"

Susan sniffed, then shook her head. "Well, I can." He rushed to the window, then gave a shout. "Bush fire, Miss Susan, bush fire! Come and have a look!"

She ran to join him at the window just as the sound of footsteps was heard outside on the veranda. Mrs. McQuarrie came hurriedly in.

"Don't let the children go out," she said swiftly to Susan, who by now was surrounded by her pupils at the window. She could now see clouds of smoke rising from behind the hills at the gully which they had visited only that morning; and from all sides of the paddocks and plains cars and men on horseback were racing towards the same spot.

"There's no danger to the homesteads," Mrs Mc-Quarrie assured Susan in reply to her look of anxious enquiry. "Wind's blowing away from us, but—" she glanced significantly at the group of children, then shook her head silently at Susan. "Now you'd better all come up to the house," she added aloud, "and I'll make a nice big pot of tea."

"Our place is out that way, Auntie Mac," said

Martin, and looked up at her with an anxious question in his eyes.

"Now, don't you worry, Mart boy," she said at once. "It doesn't look to me like a big one; and with everyone out there to beat it out, it won't spread that far. Come on now, kids, I've got some real beaut splits in the oven, just ready for eating. Come on, all of you, we'll have a feast in the kitchen."

Susan ushered the children out of the room and took another glance at the distant hills. The smell of burning was stronger now, and the air was becoming uncomfortably hot. Fortunately the children's attention had been deflected towards the kitchen 'feast' and they all raced eagerly towards the kitchen. Halfway through the rather noisy meal Susan went quietly towards the window and took another half-fearful look at the far-off smoke. Mrs McQuarrie joined her. She pointed to a travelling spark.

"That's what we've got to watch," she said in a low tone. "Just one spark could start it up here, with everything so dry. Look, there's another. Susan, you stay with the kids. I'll get Melissa and we'll fill up everything we got, just in case—" and she dashed off. But it was impossible to keep the children away from the window, and presently the six older ones were out helping Mrs McQuarrie fill jugs and baths.

"That Melissa!" she muttered to Susan during a brief interval. "She's off with the boys to help fight the fire. We could have done better with her here. The sooner she's off to her teacher's training college the better, just running wild she is since she left school. Hey!" She sniffed suddenly, and Susan, who was at the door keeping the younger children in, pointed and shouted to her,

"Look, there's a gum tree on fire, just across the track!"

"Come on!" Mrs. McQuarrie shouted to her helpers. "We got to get that out!" and presently a string of figures, headed by Martin and tailed by Mrs McQuarrie herself, was passing buckets of water along, to be thrown on the burning tree. Fortunately the fire had started on the lowest branch and Martin, who was a strong active lad, managed to climb up while the others passed jugs and buckets up to him. The smell of burning resin was strong and not unpleasant, and the fire was soon checked. The various receptacles were returned to the outhouse and the excited children trooped back on to the veranda. Mrs. McQuarrie and Susan brought out glasses of iced orange squash.

"My, but I'm enjoyin' this," James said, but Susan saw that Martin was still looking anxious.

"Here come the men!" Mary called, and pointed. Susan looked. Yes, cars and horses were coming towards the homestead, and then she heard the drone of an approaching plane.

"That's my dad's plane," said James, peering up into the sky. "Yes, it's the Cessna."

Melissa came riding up beside Ian. There were smudges of black on her face and clothes, and she carefully avoided looking at her mother.

"Hello, Ma," said Ian, "Dad's on his way, and the fire's out—right out." He looked around as he dismounted. "See you've had a bit of it here, eh?"

His father cantered up and waved to his wife. "No harm done, lass," he called as he dismounted and came up the veranda steps. "Lord knows how it started, though just a spark could do it in this dry spell. Everything O.K. here?"

"Gee, it was fun," shouted Martin, running down to meet the horses. "Here's my dad," as a shabby old car drew up.

"Well, come along in, everyone, and get the dust out of your throats," Mrs McQuarrie called, bustling her tall husband inside and beckoning to the rest of the men.

Ian moved up beside Susan.

"All right?" he asked. "Not scared? Guess it was your first bush fire, eh? As a matter of fact, it was the drop of water that's still in the gully that really put it out; that, and the beating with sticks. My, but this tea tastes good!"

Presently other parents arrived and the excited children departed for home. Melissa made tracks for one wash-house while Ian and Milton disappeared into the other. Within an hour everything was normal again except for the occasional whiff or two of burning resin borne on the night air.

"What about the barbecue?" Melissa suddenly asked as they all sat at ease on the veranda half an hour later with cups of tea or coffee and the big pot standing on a side table.

Ian stretched his long legs to their fullest extent.

"Nothing and no one's going to drag me to any barbecue to-night. Haven't you had enough of burning and—" he broke off and listened as the sound of an approaching car was heard coming nearer and nearer. "Now who the devil's this?"

Everyone straightened in their chairs and stared up the road as it stretched silvery white towards the far-off range of hills. Susan also stared with curiosity at the oncoming car, a Volkswagen, covered with dust, and driven by a man. That was all she could see as it drew up with a screech of brakes at the bottom of the steps. A silence had fallen on the group of people gathered on the veranda. Mrs McQuarrie was the first to speak, and Susan noticed the queerly apprehensive note in her voice.

"Why, it's—it's Alan!" she said, and rose to her feet.

CHAPTER 3

"HELLO there," said the newcomer, as he slammed the door of the car, then turned to look up at the group on the veranda. To Susan's sharp ears there seemed to be a slight, very slight hint of defiance in his voice. "Well, where's the fatted calf? Hello, Ma," he added as she held out her arms to him and he bent his head to hers.

"Hello, son," Susan heard her say, but the rest of the conversation, if any, was lost, in the scrape and shuffle of chairs as Ian and his father, with Melissa following, went down the steps to greet the new-comer. Susan sat where she was and listened to the low-toned voices, conscious that there was a sense of strain in the air. Presently they all came back up the steps with Alan in the midst of them.

"What about some food, Alan?" Mrs McQuarrie asked.

"No, thanks, Ma, I got a meal at the township. But I could do with a drink. Got any of the hard stuff?" There was a brief pause as Susan watched the group, and the newcomer, with eager interest. He was partly hidden by the tall figures of his father and brother. 'So this is the mysterious Alan,' she was thinking; another son. Why had no one ever mentioned the fact before?

"There's some beer in the fridge, son," she heard Mrs McQuarrie say, and then the group broke up, and Susan saw Alan McQuarrie clearly for the first time. She was surprised and rather disappointed; for he was not in the least like his father or brother. Indeed, beside Ian, Alan was almost insignificant. He was of medium height, not much taller than Susan herself; thin and spare in build and of pale indeterminate colouring.

Mrs McQuarrie suddenly said,

"Come and met Miss Susan Manley, Alan. She's the new teacher, took Kate Dunhill's place." She looked at Susan, who had risen from her chair. "Meet our younger son, from Sydney."

Susan took a step forward and held out her hand. She met the glance of a pair of pale grey eyes, and was suddenly at a loss for words—why, she did not know.

"Hi," the newcomer said briefly, and took the hand for a second, then dropped it. Without another word he followed his mother into the house.

'Well, well,' Susan thought, half angry, half amused, 'not what you'd call a friendly type!'

Pondering over the arrival of the mysterious Alan as she lay in bed that night, Susan could not curb her curiosity about him. There was something wrong here, of that she was certain. Everyone had turned very quiet for the rest of the evening and she felt sure that his arrival had been unexpected. What did he do in Sydney? she wondered. An uncouth type anyway, she decided, recalling his off-hand manner and the apology for a handshake. And yet she could not help feeling that he was up against something, somehow; and he certainly did not look like a happy person.

The next day Susan continued to ponder at intervals about Alan. He was presumably still at home, though she did not see him and no one ever mentioned him. She saw that there were several absentees from school, and she mentioned it to Mrs McQuarrie at the children's midday meal.

"Too much excitement yesterday, I guess," was the reply.

Ian came in at that moment.

"How about a ride this evening?" he suggested.

"Oh, yes, rather," smiled Susan, and he and his mother laughed at the typically English expression.

"And how's our little Pommie to-day?" said a voice from the door, and she looked over her shoulder into the pale grey eyes of Alan McQuarrie.

"Alan!" his mother said reprovingly, and smiled apologetically at Susan.

"Very well, thank you," she said, her breath seeming to come with some difficulty, then, feeling a sudden prick of irritation, she added, "What exactly does Pommie mean—if anything?"

He laughed and dragged up a chair to the table. "You wouldn't like it if I told you," he said, and grinned into her eyes.

"Then please don't use it—to me." A flush appeared in her cheek, and Ian stared at her in admiring surprise.

"Good for you, Susan!" he grinned, and cast a withering glance at his brother. Susan glanced at Alan just in time to note an expression of—what was it? She could not read what had been there for just a fleeting moment, but all at once she was sorry she had snapped at him.

"We'd better go over the yearlings this morning, Ian," Mr McQuarrie interrupted, and the conversation moved away to farming matters.

It was an apricot-and-lemon evening as Ian and Susan mounted their horses and cantered down the long drive and out on to the plain. The setting sun was touching everything with gold, and the rampart of hills in the distance was almost the colour of blood.

"We'll take the other road this time," said Ian. "It leads to the gibber country, and there you'll see some of our famous anthills. Some are about three or four times the height of a man." He glanced under Susan's wide felt hat at the bright animated face beneath. "I—I must apologise for my brother's bad manners," he added abruptly. "He's been working pretty hard."

"Oh—er—" his words had taken her by surprise, "please don't bother. He—he's not a bit like you, is he? How long is he staying?"

"Well, I don't really know. He's just finished his medical studies, and is now awaiting the final results."

"Oh," Susan said again, with a further sense of surprise. "A doctor, eh? I do hope he's successful."

"Yes, I hope so, too," Ian said, then shrugged his shoulders. "Alan's clever, but—" His tone was slightly contemptuous, Susan thought, and she began to feel vaguely sorry for the other brother.

"There's an anthill," said Ian, reining in his horse and pointing, "and this—" nodding down at the ground, "is what's called gibber country. You see, it's covered with these small stones and pebbles. Hard on the horses, so we'll tether them to this convenient tree stump. Would you like to walk over to have a closer look at the anthill?"

Susan swung a leg over the saddle. "Of course I would," she said. "I want to see just everything while I'm here."

Ian gave her a quick side glance. "Oh, but you're not thinking of going, are you?"

"No, of course not." Her colour had deepened as she spoke and she was very conscious of his presence as he walked beside her. 'How tall and handsome he is,' Susan thought, with a pleasant sense of being liked and found attractive; for her intuition told her that Ian did find her attractive. She stared at the tall ochre-coloured anthills.

"Gosh!" she said. "Why, they look exactly like tall Gothic church spires. They're really something." Ian grinned at her. "But don't they crumble away in the wet season?"

He shook his head.

"Unfortunately those seasons are so few and far between that they have time to become as hard as iron. Feel." Susan put her hand against the crenellated side of the anthill and found that it was, as Ian had said, as firm and hard as iron. She stared about her, at the blunt hills, the stony ground, the wildly untidy piles of rocks and huge boulders, and the occasional stunted skeleton of a tree. The prevailing colour was a dull reddish sepia.

"What causes it?" Susan asked, spreading her hands. "The red in everything, I mean."

"It's the minerals in the ground. Australia, as you know, is a very ancient country. That's why the hills are flat and not peaked. Millions of years of erosion has brought that about. And now geologists are just discovering that most of these hills are just full of minerals of various kinds. Take Mount Isa, for instance, which is our nearest cattle station. They've found copper, bauxite, uranium iron core, blue asbestos—the lot, as well as lead zinc and silver.

Mount Isa is the largest mining town in Australia.". He shook his head, then laughed. "It really is a fantastic town, Susan; I must take you there some time. It's got just everything, and all brought about by these mining discoveries, then there's Perth another amazing mining discovery. Ever heard of Mount Tom Price?" He grinned down at her absorbed face. "It's practically solid mineral, and every-one in Perth is making his fortune, or so they say."

"But how did it get that extraordinary name?" Susan asked.

He laughed.

"It's named after the ex-vice-president of the big steel works there. Well, shall we make a move?" Susan turned, and as she did so, something moved and scuttled away from near her. "Oh!" she exclaimed sharply, and caught hold of Ian's arm. Both his arms went quickly round her as he swung her feet clear of the ground.

"It's nothing," he said reassuringly, and set her gently on her feet again. "Look—" He pointed, and Susan stared at the ground.

"What is it?" she asked. "A lizard?"

Ian laughed, his arms still lightly clasped around her waist. "Sort of," he said. "A goanna, to be exact. They're quite harmless."

Susan laughed. "And I was just thinking how silent and deserted it all was!" she said, looking up at him.

Ian's arms fell slowly and almost reluctantly it seemed to her, from about her waist.

"The Never-Never is very deceptive," he said. "There's plenty of life here; animal, insect and reptile, under the rocks and stones; even in those half-dead-looking eucalypts. Well—" he looked at Susan and smiled half shyly, "ready for the return trip?"

On the way back Ian said to her, "We shall be starting mustering next month. You'll like to see something of that, I guess."

"Oh, yes!" Her eyes sparkled, and as she met his smiling glance, Susan suddenly thought how glad she was that she had broken free of the city and felt that she had never been so happy before.

As they came in sight of the homestead Susan saw that Alan was there sitting on the veranda rail. Ian also saw him, but said nothing as the two horses cantered up to the house and stopped. Ian led them away to the stables while Susan started to go to her own room.

"Hello there!" Alan called, and she hesitated, looking at him over her shoulder.

"Hello," she said in reply, and slowly retraced her footsteps. 'He looks lonely,' sh thought suddenly, and wondered again why everyone seemed to regard him with—distrust, was it? Or suspicion, perhaps?

"Enjoy your ride?"

Susan looked at him and saw that he was smiling, really smiling and not just grinning in a half contemptuous, half defiant fashion. And what a difference it made to his thin face! His teeth were irregular but very white; and his eyes, which had looked so pale and colourless on his arrival, with the dust of the plains upon him, were now clear and bright and shaded by thick dark lashes. 'Really quite striking,' Susan thought, as she smiled back at him. 'I feel he can be *very* nice, and exciting—when he likes.'

"Like a drink?" Alan asked, but at that moment Ian appeared at the door with two long frosted glasses on a tray. "Too late," Alan murmured, but he did not move from the rail.

Susan perched herself beside him and took the glass of orange juice from Ian and raised it to her lips.

"Umm, that's good," she said, and looked from one to the other of the two men. Ian drew up a chair to the veranda rail and sat down. A vaguely uncomfortable silence prevailed.

"Which way did you go?" Alan asked at last, but as if he were not really interested.

"North," Ian said shortly. "Towards the gibber—and the anthills." There was another short silence, then Susan asked,

"Are there many aborigines living up here?"

Alan gave a kind of bark of a laugh, and Susan glanced in surprise from him to Ian. Had she said something wrong? she wondered, for there was a closed-up look on his face. She looked at Alan and saw that he was grinning in a mirthless sort of fashion.

"No," he said, shaking his head. "And what few there are are not encouraged to stay. They're just quietly moved on."

Ian got to his feet with an impatient movement.

"Oh, don't talk rot," he said roughly. "The no-gooders are moved on, but I don't know what we'd do without the stockmen, as you very well know. Well—" he stretched his shoulders, "it's me for a shower. How about you, Sue? Tea's not very far off."

"Yes, I could certainly do with a shower." She slid from the veranda rail, and went down the steps. "See you both later." She was glad to get away from the antagonistic atmosphere that always seemed to be between these two brothers.

However, Alan did not appear for the evening meal, and Susan was glad that he did not. There was always such an uncomfortable feeling prevailing whenever he was around. No one remarked on his absence and the evening was passed in the usual fashion, chatting to each other and listening to some new records which Melissa had just received from Townsville. Susan thought once or twice that Mrs McQuarrie, or Auntie Mac as she had told Susan to call her, was unusually silent, and once she noticed an expression of sadness on her face. Susan wondered for how long Alan would be staying at home. If he were waiting for examination results it could be some weeks, she thought, then dismissed him from her mind.

Life soon slipped into a pleasant routine for Susan. She found her job interesting with children who were eager to learn, and Susan herself learnt quite a lot from them. Life on a cattle station was quiet and placid for the womenfolk, but Susan had never been a girl for the bright lights. She discovered that Kanoch Doon homestead had a good and quite extensive library, and when the long cool evenings were not spent on the veranda, talking, listening to the radio and sometimes dancing to the record player, she was quite happy to sit in her own comfortable room reading or marking the children's exercise books. Also a pleasant friendship was slowly developing between herself and Ian. He was a quiet, matter-of-fact sort of person, rather reserved, but Susan soon found him to be a fund of interesting and stimulating information. He had lived all his life in North Queensland and seemed to know all about the fauna and flora of the Outback—though, as Susan had to admit, she herself knew so little that his knowledge might have just seemed extensive. But the fact remained that there were few questions she put to him to which he did not know the answer. For instance, there was the day when they had gone riding again towards the hills and Susan had noticed and pointed out to Ian the busy little bird moving about among some acacia shrubs.

"That's a bower bird," he had told her. "He builds himself a boudoir of flowers and leaves."

"A nest?" Susan had asked, but Ian had shaken his head.

"Not a nest," he said, "just a bower. He arranges it in a pretty pattern, then he fusses round and re-arranges it—just like a woman fixing a bowl of flowers in her sitting room."

Susan stared at him, then laughed.

"Why does he do it? Courting?"

Ian shrugged. "Your guess is as good as mine," he said. "Perhaps he's like the woman, he just wants to see beauty in his home—or again he may be bored, and it's something to do."

"Oh," sighed Susan, "now you've gone and spoilt it all!"

Then there was the other occasion, this time in the gibber when Susan's sharp eyes had seen something move among the rocks.

"Look, Ian," she said, pointing, "it's a cat, surely. What can it be doing out here?"

Ian's eyes followed her pointing finger and presently he said,

"You're right, Sue, it is a cat, but a wild one. They're called quolls—not many of them about."

Susan was enchanted on another evening expedition at her first sight of a dingo or wild dog.

"But he's quite beautiful," she said, studying the creature as he stood watching them from behind a tree. "His eyes are the same colour as his coat—real amber."

"Yes," Ian agreed. "He's certainly a handsome feller, but if I had a gun I'd—" and then at her look of shocked protest, he described to Susan the amount of damage done by the dingoes on a cattle station. "I guess you'd not feel so indignant," he concluded, "if you came across the carcase of a lamb or a calf which he'd just savaged."

She nodded. "No," she said soberly, "I'm quite sure I wouldn't, but—well, I am rather glad you didn't bring a gun."

Ian laughed. "Well, all right," he said. "But you know, life here in the Never-Never is very primitive. It's a case of the survival of the fittest, and the dingoes know it, and so does everything else."

On a third occasion Ian pointed out the mound of a mallee fowl and described how the bird digs, then lays its eggs well under the soil. The male bird uncovers them every day to test their temperature, then covers them up again.

"Where is the mother bird while all this is going on?" Susan enquired.

"Oh, she's done her job in laying the eggs," Ian explained. "When the chicks are hatched out they have to dig their own way to the surface of the ground and then fend for themselves. And Nature sees that there are not too many survivors," he concluded dryly.

As time went on Susan began to be quite knowledgeable herself. She was able after a time to pick out the various eucalyptus trees, having been previously told by Ian that there were nearly fifty of them, and the day when she identified an Antarctic beech with its enormous bole she began to feel that she was really one with the land of the Never-Never.

Though Susan knew that Alan was still officially at home she saw very little of him. Every evening he went off either on horseback or in one of the cars and disappeared into the night, and she never saw or heard him return. But one evening, when she had finished correcting the children's exercise books, she wandered out into the nearest paddock for a breath of cool air before going to bed. Suddenly there was a movement quite close to where she stood, then a figure appeared from round the corner of the nearby veranda.

"Hello," said a voice very softly, and Susan's heart gave a queer little jump. She had recognised the voice as belonging to Alan, but, knowing so little of him, and that not exactly to his advantage, she felt distinctly on her guard. "It's only me," he went on, coming a little nearer so that she could just see the outline of his face. "I hope I didn't scare you."

"No—" Her voice sounded slightly breathless, "no, you didn't scare me. I—I just wondered for the moment who it was." She saw the gleam of his teeth as he smiled.

"And you don't mind?" he asked. "I mean, coming here, and—talking to you?"

"Why, of course not," she said, composure returning to her with a rush. "Why should I mind? Anyway, this is *your* home."

"Yes—well—" His voice sounded cynical and she

saw his shoulders shrug. "Cigarette?" he asked, taking a packet from his pocket and holding it out to her. Susan took one and he lit it and then his own. There was a short but friendly sort of silence between them, then Alan said,

"D'you like the life here, Susan? It occurs to me that it must be very different from everything you've been used to."

"Yes, it is." Her voice was soft and thoughtful. "But I like it. It's so big, and—" she looked about her, then back at him, "so quiet and peaceful. I like it because it *is* so different from everything I've ever known, the cities and towns, and—" she paused.

"So you don't care for the life of the big cities?"

"Well—" Susan paused again, "I don't really know, I've been here for such a short time; but somehow I felt much more lonely in Adelaide than ever I've done here, even though I had my friend Pat with me—my girl friend, I mean."

"What's happened to her?"

Susan smiled in the darkness.

"She's getting married quite soon. She met someone in Adelaide just after we arrived." There was another pause, then Alan said, and she could almost hear the laugh in his voice,

"Perhaps that will be happening to you, too."

Susan laughed a trifle self-consciously. "Well, I suppose it could, but I'm in no hurry."

"Wise girl," he said lightly. "Though you won't have far to look when you do get round to it."

She glanced quickly at him and wished that she could see the expression of his face, for there seemed to her to be a slightly questioning note in his voice. She drew on her cigarette and waited.

"Well," Alan said at last, "I'm glad to hear that you're not lonely here in Kangaroo. They're a friendly crowd, and brother Ian looks after you, I guess."

Susan smiled to herself. "Yes, they are all friendly," she said. "And they do—look after me, as you put it." She waited for his reply.

"Yes, well—" he said, paused, then added abruptly, "I shall be leaving for Sydney soon. I—I wondered if you—" but at that moment Ian's voice came across to them from the house.

"That you, Susan?" he called, his voice sounding pleasantly resonant in the night stillness. "Come up and have a nightcap."

She looked at Alan. He hesitated for a moment, then laughed in a slightly defiant way.

"Yes, come on," he said to her, "let's both go up. I'm sure my big brother would be delighted to see—us."

Susan looked straight at him. The moon was riding high in the heavens by now and his face was clearly visible. The expression on it matched his voice for defiance. But as his eyes met hers, it slowly changed to a kind of weary misery.

"Sorry," he muttered. "I shouldn't have said that to you. Forget it. You go up, Susan, and I'll—" and before she could think of anything to say in return, he had stepped back quickly and was gone round a corner of the building.

Susan stared after him for a moment, then turned and walked slowly up to the house. She was beginning to feel vaguely sorry for Alan, for she sensed that he was unhappy. What was wrong between him and the rest of the family? she wondered. Ian came down the veranda steps to meet her.

"I thought I heard voices out there," he said, looking at her questioningly, but Susan was spared the necessity of replying by Mrs McQuarrie, who had just appeared at the door.

"Tea up!" she called. "But you can have something else if you like; it's all in the fridge. Susan, Ian—?"

"What for you, Dad?" Ian called to his father, who was just coming round from the back veranda. "Beer?"

"Beer it is, son." Son, Susan thought, and reflected that she had never once heard Douglas McQuarrie address Alan as 'son'.

"Not much point in making tea," observed Mrs McQuarrie. "Susan, how about you?" She glanced round the veranda. "Where's Melissa? Ah, here she is. Where have you been, Melissa? You ought to be doing some study, you know."

"I'll have tea, please, Auntie Mac," said Susan, perching herself on the veranda rail. Ian leant against it beside her. Melissa strolled over to join them, looking cross and out of sorts.

"This study business," she muttered. "I'm fed up with it—and with Ma." She paused and looked at Susan. "Has she told you about the get-together to-morrow?"

Susan shook her head.

"What's a get-together?" she asked.

"Oh, so she hasn't got round to it yet. Well, it's the club afternoon; the Outback Wives' Club. Ever heard of it?"

Susan looked at her with bright, interested eyes.

"No," she said. "Do tell me about it, Melissa, it sounds interesting."

"You'll soon know all about it, Sue," Ian cut in with a laugh. "Here's Mother bearing down upon us now. I bet——"

"Susan dear," Mrs McQuarrie said as she came up to the little group, "I meant to tell you before this about to-morrow, but there were so many things—anyway, it's our club afternoon."

"Club?" Susan asked, mystified. "Melissa was just starting to tell me about it. Who do you have for members?"

"Members?" There was a combined laugh from the other three. "Well—" Mrs McQuarrie continued, "we've got—let me see now, yes, there are five hundred and forty-seven up to now."

Susan stared at her, then at the other two.

"But where do they all come from?" she asked.

"They come from all over the Outback in Queensland, Western Australia and the Northern Territory." Then as Susan continued to stare at her in puzzled wonderment, Mrs McQuarrie laughed and said, "It's the Outback Wives' Club of the Air, and their voices come here, over the air—something like your school of the air."

"Oh!" Enlightenment began to dawn upon her. "I think I see now, but——"

"Well now," Mrs McQuarrie interrupted, "we have a meeting to-morrow afternoon, and I'd like fine for you to come. It's just after school, and Kate Dunhill used to finish lessons a bit early. All right?"

"Yes, I'd love to come," Susan agreed eagerly. "Do tell me more about it."

"Here, sit down, Ma," said Ian, pulling a chair

forward. "Tell the lassie all she wants to know about the galah club."

"Now, Ian, it's not all galah," said his mother. "It's only natural the women should want to chat to each other when they get the chance." She turned to Susan and answered her glance of enquiry. "The men call it the galah session because of the chatter. Perhaps you haven't yet come across the galah bird, very pretty, with pink and white plumage, but it's an awful chatterbox, so—"

"Yes, I see now," Susan said, laughing. "But do tell me more about the club, Auntie Mac. It sounds most interesting, quite unique, I should think."

"I guess it's that all right." She settled herself comfortably in her chair. "Fetch me another cup of tea, Ian," she said to her son. "Well, dear," she turned to Susan, "as I said, it's the Women's Club of the Air, and the members are just anyone who's got a transceiver, or is near to someone who has."

"Sounds like a sort of Women's Institute of the Air," Susan observed.

"Yes, well, we call them the country-women's clubs out here."

"Who actually runs it?"

Mrs. McQuarrie took the refilled cup from Ian, then turned again to Susan.

"It's run from the Royal Flying Doctor Base at Alice Springs, just as the School of the Air is. It starts at a quarter to four and goes on to four-thirty or thereabouts, and it's held on the first Wednesday of the month. Of course we do have some members who are able to attend in person. Most of your pupils' mothers come, so—" she burst into a hearty laugh, "the first Wednesday in the month is a real old field day, I can tell you. Well, what do you think of it?"

"Oh, I'd love to come! I could give you a hand with—do you have a break for tea?"

"Yes, just for five minutes. You see, with only three-quarters of an hour at our disposal, time is valuable, and five minutes is all we can allow ourselves."

"Yes, I see, but—well, why have it?" Susan asked. "It does seem that with—"

"Yes, I know," Mrs McQuarrie interrupted, nodding her head. "It's kinda psychological, I guess. But it was put to the vote once and we found that all, or nearly all, of the members wanted the tea break to stay. The women said it made them feel chummy-like, as if it was a real-life club with everyone sitting and drinking cups of tea at exactly the same time; a sort of link. See what I mean?"

Susan nodded thoughtfully. "Yes, I see exactly what you mean," she said. "I'm looking forward to it, and I'd like to help, too."

And the next day, the first Wednesday in the month, the fun started. Several of the mothers who lived not too far out came over in the morning with their children and spent the day with Mrs McQuarrie and Melissa baking cakes for the afternoon's events. Susan became infected with the prevailing excitement and bustle, and waited impatiently for school to end. As soon as lunch was over several cars arrived with club members who had travelled many miles across country to attend the meeting in person. And well before three-forty-five, everyone, including Susan, was seated in the big schoolroom in front of the transceiver. Tongues wagged non-stop as questions and answers catapulted between guests. All were interested in meeting Susan—a new face—but particularly the mothers who made interested enquiries as to their children's progress. Sharp at three-forty-five Mrs McQuarrie threw the switch on the face of the transceiver, and almost at once a clear woman's voice came through.

"Hello, members," it said. "Ready for our theme song? Then off we go!" and there was the sudden sound of a piano thumping out the tune of "Waltzing Matilda". Everyone joined in with gusto. At the conclusion of the song, the president bade everyone welcome, then called upon the secretary to read the minutes of the last meeting.

A tape recorder was used here. After the reading of the minutes was over there came the highlight of the meeting—personal news of homes and families; and this, Susan guessed, was what Ian had called the galah session. A full quarter of an hour was allowed for it, and then the guest speaker was announced. He was a Methodist Minister from the Australian Inland Mission. He spoke for about ten minutes about the work of the A.I.M. in Arnhem Land and spoke very well, too.

At the end of the talk the secretary announced a five-minute break for tea. Mrs. McQuarrie and several of the other women immediately left the room, but within seconds were back carrying trays of tea and biscuits which must have been all ready waiting, prepared, Susan knew, by Melissa. Chatter and laughter was now well under weigh, both in the room and over the air. At the conclusion of the stipulated five minutes trays were swiftly removed and the noise died down. Mrs McQuarrie turned again to the transceiver as the voice of the secretary came through once more. She announced that a competition had been arranged for the next meeting. All members were asked to bake a fruit cake, weight and price specified, which was to be judged and points awarded by other members chosen by the chairman or president. Not an easy task, Susan thought, when one considers that the members of the Club of the Air are scattered over the great Interior for hundreds of miles.

By the time the details of the competition had been given out and taken down on the tape recorder it was four-thirty, and time to close the meeting. Susan thought she had never known an hour to flash past so quickly. Amid a chorus of goodbyes over the air, the members gathered at Kanoch Doon began to make preparation for departure.

Later that same evening, after the usual hearty 'tea' of steak, eggs and bread and butter, helped down by the inevitable large pot of tea, Susan asked Mrs McQuarrie for some more details of this unique W.I. of the air.

"I just loved it all, Auntie Mac," she said, perching herself on her favourite spot on the veranda rail, "but I just wondered—it was while the guest speaker was on—if you have a subscription for membership."

"Oh yes, we certainly do. Everyone pays a yearly sub, and we have special times, usually during the galah session—" she laughed, "I shouldn't call it that, I know—when we discuss ways of spending the money to best advantage. A tenth of the fund is always put aside for charities; then a certain amount each month is put by to buy more transceivers for yet more lonely isolated spots."

"How much do the transceivers cost?" Susan enquired.

"Round about a hundred pounds," was the reply. "Then there's the fee and travelling expenses of the speakers; not that they ever ask for much. In fact we have a job to make them take even the money for the travelling expenses. But we always insist that they're not actually out of pocket. Then there's the get-togethers. We hold them just once a year and they usually take the form of races, a barbecue and a party. That costs quite a lot and needs a great deal of organising. You see, it means camping for at least one night, sometimes more. Husbands, boy-friends, parents, all are invited. Yes, the get-togethers are very popular; I wouldn't miss them for worlds."

"My, oh, my," said Susan, "the Wives' Club of the Air is quite something, isn't it? What other competitions do you have?"

"We—there's the exchange recipe. That always goes down well. Oh, and the 'do-it-yourself' contests are also very popular, I suppose because life in the Outback *is* do-it-yourself or go without." She laughed, then added, "Sometimes we go all cultured, and have general knowledge contests or poetry quotations."

Susan smiled. "Which do you think is the most popular of all your activities?" she asked.

Mrs McQuarrie burst into hearty laughter in which her husband and Ian joined.

"Now what do *you* think?" she asked, and then replied to her own question. "The galah session, of course. It's personal, you see, little tit-bits of information from everyone's everyday lives that you can ask questions about and carry on till the next meeting if you know what I mean." Susan nodded. "It's like gradually getting to know all the family; names and ages of the kids, and the things they say, the exasperating habits of someone else's husband. Things like that, you know."

Susan nodded again, then caught Ian's eye.

"Well, all the galahs have gone home to their nests," he remarked with a grin. "So how about a little stroll in the paddock, Sue?"

"Yes, all right." She slid from the rail, and as they started down the veranda steps she caught the fleeting look of gratification on Mrs McQuarrie's face. Susan's own face was thoughtful as she strolled beside Ian down the garden path towards the gate leading to the nearest paddock. She thought she knew what was in Auntie Mac's mind. That it was high time Ian married, and that here at last was a girl that he seemed to fancy and a girl who presumably liked this life on a cattle station. After all, Susan thought, it wouldn't be every girl's choice, too quiet for most. She glanced sideways at Ian and found that he was watching her.

"Well—" he said softly, "so you enjoyed your afternoon?"

She nodded and smiled up at him. "Yes, it was really interesting. I'd never heard of a club of the air before, but I think it's a marvellous idea. I wonder who first thought it up."

"I wouldn't really know, but it's certainly very popular with the womenfolk, and I guess it's made a big difference to their lives." He paused for a moment, then observed in a slightly awkward tone of voice, "you seem to be settling down very well here in Kangaroo. Still liking it?"

"Oh yes, I'm loving it all, every bit of it," Susan

told him, wondering suddenly what had happened to Letty lately. There was another short pause, then Ian said abruptly,

"But not for always, though, I guess?" He looked straight in front of him as he spoke.

"Well—" Susan said rather uncertainly, "I—er—it's a bit early to say, isn't it? I've been here only—how long? Four weeks, but I do like it, and—" she was feeling distinctly flustered and was glad when Ian changed the subject by saying,

"We'll be starting cattle mustering soon. You'd like to see something of that, I expect."

"Oh, would I?" said Susan, then she laughed and added, "I want to see just everything!"

Ian laughed too, then looked up at the sound of galloping hooves in the distance. On the horizon was a cloud of dust which drew rapidly nearer and then as the horse approached them Susan saw that it was Alan. He drew up beside them, doffed his hat to Susan, then regarded his brother with a mocking smile. Susan noticed that his slightly overlapping teeth gave to his mouth a queer puckish twist when he smiled.

"Well, well!" he drawled, and waved his hand round at the scene—distant hills, tinged with the rose and gold of the setting sun, and over all a dream-like blue haze which hovered over the grassy plains and paddocks. The few trees and low bushes scattered around appeared to be swimming rootless in the darkening landscape. "A perfect setting for romance, don't you agree, Ian?"

"I hadn't thought of it like that." His voice was short, and Alan laughed.

"You always were an old stick-in-the-mud," he

observed. "It must be very frustrating—to the girl of the moment." Ian's face became a dull red, but Susan stared straight at Alan.

"What a load of rubbish you talk," she said. "You're just a silly little schoolboy."

He stared at her for a moment, and the surprise on his face was quite ludicrous. Then he burst out laughing, and, after a pause, Ian joined in. Susan looked at them both, then she too joined in the general hilarity.

"Well, well!" Alan said at last. "D'you know, brother, I think the lass may be right," and he glanced at Ian with one eyebrow quirked up at an enquiring angle. Ian shrugged, the lines of laughter still crinkling the corners of his blue eyes. Susan's remark seemed to have, temporarily at least, cleared away the dark cloud which seemed to be always between these brothers. Somehow she had succeeded in debunking them both—for the moment anyway. Alan looked down at her and grinned again.

"I guess I'd better be on my way home," he said. "Oh, and in case I don't see you again, Susan, I'll say cheerio."

She stared up at him in surprise, and so did Ian.

"But where are you going?" she asked. "You'll be here to-morrow, won't you?"

Ian was still looking mystified.

"I thought you were staying at home till you'd heard your results," he said.

"Yes, that's right." Alan's voice was off-hand, almost casual. "I heard this evening. It's—O.K."

"Congratulations," Ian said at once, and Susan echoed him with,

"Oh, that's splendid news, Alan! My congratulations too. I bet your mum and dad are thrilled."

A peculiar expression crossed his face. "Yes, I guess so," he said slowly. "Yes, things'll be much—easier for Ma now."

Susan stared at him, puzzled, then glanced at Ian and saw that his lips were set in a hard straight line as he stared up at his brother.

"Oh, why can't you forget the whole thing? Put it behind you," he burst out. "Dad has, I'm sure."

"I'll bet he has," was the swift reply. "Just put awkward things behind you and out of sight; that's his way, and—" He stopped, and Susan felt sure that he had been about to add 'yours, too'. There was an angry silence in which she felt acutely uncomfortable and suddenly irritated with these two brothers.

"Oh, come on," she snapped suddenly at Ian. "What's the matter with you both? Whatever it is, why don't you have it out, and settle it—or bury it once and for all?"

They stared into her flushed face and challenging eyes, then Alan drawled,

"This girl's full of common sense. Well, well!" He picked up the reins from the horse's neck. " 'Bye, Susan, be seeing you again—some time—I hope." He gave her a mock salute, wheeled his horse round, and galloped off in a cloud of dust.

Ian looked at Susan.

"Look, girl," he said, "I'm sorry about all that, but—"

"But nothing," she interrupted him impatiently. "I'm not interested in your private family feuds, Ian, but, like I said, it seems a pity that you can't somehow settle your differences, at your ages. However, from now on, I don't suppose you'll be seeing much of each other. I mean—" she paused, and Ian nodded slowly.

"Perhaps it's a good thing, the only thing," he said at last, "and of course, I'm honestly delighted at Alan's news. I—wonder what he'll do now."

Susan stared at him in bewilderment.

"But don't you know *anything* about your brother's future plans?" she asked.

Ian shrugged his shoulders.

"Well," he said at last, "I guess, with his degree, which I suppose is what he meant by 'It's O.K.', he'll be starting his own practice somewhere or go into a hospital; I don't know much about these things."

"But—" Susan was starting again, but changed her mind. This family quarrel had evidently gone very deep, and she did not want to seem to invite Ian's confidence. Naturally, she was curious; who wouldn't be? she thought, but this was not the time, or the place, and it was none of her business anyway. "We'd better be getting back, Ian," she said instead, and turned away from him. "It's getting chilly."

That evening the family gathered on the veranda as usual. There was no sign of Alan, so Susan concluded that he had already gone. Melissa started the record player and Ian drew Susan to her feet and started to dance. She found him rather awkward on his feet and she did not really enjoy it, and neither did he, Susan was sure.

"I wonder where Letty is these days," Melissa said, and glanced sideways at Ian. He made no reply, and all at once there was the sound of an approaching car. Everyone looked towards the paddock gates and Melissa laughed and said, "Talk of the devil! Hi, Letty!"

The car turned in at the gates and drew up with a skirl of gravel at the wide veranda steps. Susan looked as Letty climbed out and just for a fleeting second she caught the glance of her eye as she looked up at Ian, then at herself. 'Yes,' Susan thought uncomfortably, 'this girl has marked out Ian for her own, and she's jealous.' She glanced at Ian, but he was changing the record. Letty came up the steps as Melissa went to meet her. Mrs McQuarrie came from the house at the same moment carrying a tray with coffee-pot, tea-pot and biscuits. Susan thought she regarded Letty a trifle impatiently.

"Hello, Letty," she said. "How are you? Well, sit down, lass."

Everyone sat down and Ian came strolling back. He sat down again by Susan, and Letty looked at him with heightened colour. Melissa gave a little giggle, then went to help her mother with the tray.

"Oh, I met Alan not so long ago," Letty suddenly said. "He told me he was returning to Sydney tonight. Has he gone already?"

For a moment no one spoke, then Mrs McQuarrie said hurriedly,

"Yes—yes, that's right, Letty. He hasn't long been gone." As she spoke there was an abrupt movement from where the boss was sitting; and as Susan glanced at him for a moment she felt almost certain that this bit of news had come as a complete surprise to him and that he had not known till this moment that his younger son had left Kanoch Doon. Susan's eyes turned to Ian's face and she saw that he was looking rather angrily at his mother. "Yes—" Mrs

McQuarrie's voice now sounded nervous and flustered as she still bent over the tray of cups and saucers. "Yes—er—Alan left about an hour ago. You'll be pleased to know that he's been successful in his exams." Susan saw her look pleadingly at her husband, and she just caught the apologetic murmur about not yet having had the opportunity, etc., etc. Her husband's face was like a thundercloud as he sat there without paying attention to her faltering words and pleading looks.

Letty had by now sensed the discomfort in the atmosphere, but had only a vague idea as to the cause. She suddenly jumped impatiently to her feet and turned to Ian.

"Come on, Ian," she said, "how about a dance with me? And it's no use saying you can't dance, because I saw you just now. Go on, Melissa, put a record on, please." So the uncomfortable moment passed, and after half an hour or so Ian drove with Letty out to the paddock gates to put her on her way. Susan seized the opportunity to say her goodnights and slipped off to bed.

She lay awake for some time, wondering again about this family with whom she was now living. It seemed obvious that the quarrel or rift was between Alan on one side and the rest of the family on the other, though Susan did not feel so sure about Mrs McQuarrie. Something must have happened in the past, she thought, something really very serious, too. Something which Alan had done, perhaps, and which had aroused the deep anger or resentment of his father and brother. Now what, Susan thought, would be most likely to arouse the anger of this arrogant and very ancestor-proud big landowner? Some blow to his dignity or pride, perhaps. Susan called Alan to mind and decided that it would not be difficult to imagine him doing that. Alan was very much one of the younger generation; the past meant little or nothing to him. And the boss was—well, almost archaic. But what of Ian? Well, he was very like his father in some ways. Susan had sensed that he was proud, and perhaps a little intolerant. Anyway, she thought, why shouldn't a man be proud of his ancestry? And the McQuarries certainly had something to be proud of, for Melissa had told her that the family was distantly related to that of Governor McQuarrie. Susan began to feel drowsy and gave up the problem of the McQuarrie family feud.

CHAPTER 4

THE next day nothing was said of Alan's departure. Douglas McQuarrie was his usual rather aloof self, but Susan thought his wife's face bore a slightly different expression. Ian was rather quiet, too. Melissa was the only member of the family who appeared to be unaffected by the previous evening's events. Indeed she appeared to be bubbling over with a suppressed excitement. When evening came Ian did not suggest a walk or ride to Susan and went off early to bed. Melissa and Milton were whispering together at one end of the veranda while Susan sat with Mrs McQuarrie. The whole atmosphere seemed changed all at once, and she was glad when the evening came to an end and she was able to say goodnight and go to her own room. 'What's wrong with Ian?' Susan wondered in a depressed fashion as she got into bed and snapped off her light.

However, the next day all seemed back to normal. Mrs McQuarrie was her usual placid self and Ian greeted Susan at breakfast with his pleasant smile and a cheery question as to what she was doing that evening. Life slipped back into its quietly happy tempo and Alan appeared to be forgotten, or at least relegated to the past. So far as Susan could gather he did not write to any of his family, even his mother. Only once did Mrs McQuarrie mention him, and that quite casually to Susan when they happened to be alone together in the kitchen.

Curiosity had driven Susan to enquire how Alan was faring.

"Oh, he's all right," was the reply. "He's not a chap for writing much, never was, but he knows what he wants *and* he'll go for it. We'll get news, in Alan's own time."

One morning Susan had an invitation to visit Alice Springs. It came over the air just as school had started. Susan stared in excited surprise at the transceiver as the voice came through. It said, 'Miss Susan Manley of Kanoch Doon Cattle station is invited to spend any week-end during the next month with Mrs Ferguson of the staff of the School of the Air at Alice Springs in order to discuss the forthcoming get-together party for the pupils of the School of the Air. Just give me a few days' notice. Over.'

Susan was thrilled, particularly as Ian immediately offered to drive her over to the Alice, even though the cattle mustering would have started.

"Would the week-end after next suit you?" he asked her. "Then, next Saturday, as there's no school, you'll be able to come with Melissa for the first day." He laughed and looked down into Susan's bright face. "I guess one day will be enough too; it's heat and dust and flies most of the time. We'll go in the ute and when we get to the first camp, I can pick up horses from one of the stockmen. It means staying the night, so you two girls can share a tent. Will that suit you, or——" he looked at her uncertainly, "did you want to go for the conference in town earlier than Saturday week?"

"No, oh no, that'll be fine," Susan hastened to assure him. "I couldn't bear to miss the mustering, and she did say any week-end during the next month.

Thanks a lot, Ian, for offering to take me in. Oh!" she laughed excitedly. "So many thrilling things seem to be happening to me all at once. I'm so glad I left Adelaide, though it's a nice town—I mean city."

Ian laughed. "Well, well, you're certainly appreciative of our outback," he remarked. "It's a real pleasure to show you around, Sue. I—er—hope you'll be here for a long time yet."

"So do I. Gosh," she gave an excited little skip, "I can hardly wait for Saturday, and then the Saturday after that." He laughed again and threw an affectionate arm round Susan's shoulders.

Saturday morning arrived, and Susan and Melissa packed in beside Ian in the utility. The sun was just rising behind the distant hills and beginning to stain the rolling plains and paddocks with a warm golden light. Wisps of purplish mist still lingered in the hollows of the hills. As the car came out of the big main gate and turned left on the bitumen road, Ian suddenly pointed and said,

"Look, Susan, over there. Now that's something you don't often see now, they're dying out fast."

Susan looked and saw a ramshackle old cart drawn by two horses. All she could see of the driver was a wide battered old felt hat with beneath it a glimpse of bushy grey whisker. Tethered to the cart and trotting smartly along behind it were a couple of tough-looking dogs.

"What does *he* do for a living?" Susan asked. "Or is he just a sort of tramp, a swagman, they're called, aren't they?"

"No, he's not a swagman," Ian said, grinning, "and there aren't many of those left either. No, this chap is a sheep and cattle drover. He goes from one station to another moving the animals to the cattle market. It's contract work. He always has a couple of dogs with him, sometimes more. I think this chap is a sheep drover; you can tell by his dogs, kelpies or border collies. If it were cattle he'd be using blue heelers. He couldn't do without his dogs. They're tireless and completely dependable. But he belongs to a past era, like the 'jolly swagman'. The enormously long articulated trains—cattle trains, I mean—are used now. They can take the animals to the market towns in a few days, whereas in the old days it would take weeks, sometimes months, for the drovers to get them there. And you can imagine the poor condition they'd be in after all that driving over all sorts of country." Ian slowed down as they passed the cart and waved to the driver.

They continued on their way and presently Ian pointed again. "Here comes a cattle train," he said. "We'd better give it a wide berth."

Susan stared, but all she could see was a cloud of dust on the flat horizon. It came rapidly nearer and Ian veered as far out as he could. As the cattle train passed them Susan stared at the long procession of articulated trucks covered with canvas awnings.

"Phew!" said Melissa, fanning herself vigorously as she gazed after the last swaying truck. "I suppose they're on their way to the cattle market at Mount Isa."

Susan could hear the bellowing of the animals and could not help feeling sorry for them. It was nearing midday and the sun was high in the sky before the utility arrived at the camp in the foothills. The aborigine stockmen, all in their gay checked shirts, were already there with Milton, the jackeroo.

"These abos are fine horsemen," Ian told Susan. "They can do just anything on a horse, almost part of it."

There was the usual camp fire going with a big steaming billy swinging over it. After a picnic lunch tents were erected. The girls had a short rest, and then mounted the horses which had been brought out by the stockmen. Led by Melissa, the two girls followed Ian and Milton to a spot between two lofty outcrops of rock where they would have a clear view of the proceedings. Susan stared in breathless wonder at the scene spread out before her. The galloping horses, the shouting stockmen in their gay reds and yellows, the pounding cattle, and the racing, barking dogs.

"This is only the first mustering camp," Melissa told her. "There are ten altogether, and the whole area for mustering takes in about seventy miles."

"Seventy miles!" echoed Susan. "But for heaven's sake, how long does this mustering take?"

"Oh, about three months. There are thousands of head of cattle, you know; and once outside the paddocks they can wander at will in search of fodder and water. Sometimes they breed with the wild bulls, and then—" she laughed, and looked at Susan. "I'd love you to see a wild bull being rounded up, and quite a number of them are. The stockman has first to throw him with the rope, then leap on to the bull's back, get the rope round his legs. He then has to sit on top of him while he brands and castrates him, poor old chap."

Susan started at her with open mouth. "Well—" she said at last, and Melissa laughed again, "I—I guess I'll take your word for it, Melissa, but I'd hate to see it."

"Thought you were all for life in the wide open spaces," Melissa remarked with a grin. "It's not all pearly mornings and apricot sunsets by any means. You've got to take the rough with the smooth, that's if you intend to stay."

"You have to take the rough with the smooth anywhere," Susan replied, meeting Melissa's slightly teasing glance. She could feel her cheeks warming under the younger girl's gaze, but Melissa said no more. Susan's eyes turned again towards the scene below. She could just make out the figure of Milton at the far side of the bellowing mob—but there was no sign of Ian. Susan continued to stare enthralled at the novel scene, and did not notice that Melissa was not still with her. When she did look round to say something to her she found the other girl had vanished. She stared about her, but there was no sign of Melissa or the horse. Ian and Milton had joined the throng below some time ago, and now Susan began to wonder if she could find her own way back to camp. She waited a few more minutes in case Melissa returned, then wheeled her horse. As she did so a loud rending sound came to her ears and she stared at a clump of wattle from which the sound seemed to have come. Was Melissa in trouble? she wondered, keeping tight hold of the horse's reins. She thought she saw something move and waited with held breath. There was still no sign of Melissa and suddenly Susan felt very alone. She turned her head and looked down into the gully, but all she could see was a mob of tossing horns. The stockmen all seemed to have moved out of sight—and the sun was beginning to set. Susan decided to move—then the something behind the wattle seemed to explode into the air; and at the same moment Susan's horse gave a shrill whinny of fright and bolted.

As she clutched wildly at the reins Susan had a lightning glimpse of a huge kangaroo bounding from one rock to another and away down the slope. She hung on frantically to the horse's reins, and then, to her heartfelt relief, she heard the hoofs of another horse pounding along behind her.

"Susan!" It was Melissa's voice calling to her. "It's O.K., I'll head him off." She glanced sideways and saw that Melissa's mount was coming in from the side in a wide circle. Susan gripped the horse with her knees and hung on to the reins with all her strength and slowly she felt the horse responding. It began to slow down and the two horses came to a halt almost nose to nose. Susan's heart was pounding and she was trembling all over, but somehow she managed to smile at Melissa.

"Heavens, what happened?" the latter asked. "I slipped off behind a rock to—have a word with Milton, and when I got back there you were galloping off into the unknown. What happened, Susan?"

Susan grinned as she flexed her aching arm muscles.

"Oh, just a kangaroo," she said as casually as she could. "It suddenly leapt out from behind that wattle, quite near, as you see. The horse took fright and bolted. Still—" she shrugged and grinned again, "you've got to take the rough with the smooth, I guess."

Melissa looked at her and took a deep breath. "Well," she said, "it gave me a fright, I don't mind telling you. I think we'd better not tell Ian about this, Sue, d'you mind? He'd blame me for not looking after you. You see, I'm of the opinion that brother Ian has fallen for you."

Susan felt her cheeks going hot. "Oh, I don't think so," she said. "I—I like Ian, but we're just—"

"Just good friends, like all those film stars, eh?" Melissa grinned.

"Of course there's no need to mention it to Ian," Susan said, ignoring Melissa's comment, then she added, "Anyway, why was it so important to see Milton just then?"

"Oh," Melissa turned her face away from Susan's eyes, "he—er—he's advising me about—something. Anyway, I still think I'm right about Ian, and I guess that's why Letty hasn't been over lately."

Susan began to feel rather annoyed.

"Don't be silly," she said. "There's nothing like that—and I hardly know Letty French. We'd better get back, hadn't we, before someone comes to look for us."

On the way back Melissa suddenly asked,

"What do you think of Alan, my younger brother?"

Susan was silent. She was reluctant to discuss Alan with another member of the family.

"Well," she said evasively at last, "I hardly saw anything of him while he was home. He seemed— all right to me."

"Alan's a good cobber," said Melissa. "You can take it from me. I don't know what the row's about, but I bet it's Dad's fault, he has to have his own way—and Ma's nearly as bad."

Susan looked at Melissa's round childish face and

smiled. She was the first one to say anything good of Alan, she thought, and liked her for it.

When the two girls arrived back at the camp they found Ian just preparing to come and meet them.

"You're late," he greeted Melissa, with his eyes on Susan. "I was beginning to think something had happened to you."

"Of course not," she replied airily. "What could happen?"

"Lots. Well, anyway, come along. Food's just ready." He turned to Susan. "Enjoyed your day?"

"Marvellous!" She could smell the delicious aroma of steak and sausages being cooked over the camp fire, and realised after a whole day in the open air just how hungry she could get. Everyone gathered round the fire with piled-up plates on their knees and steaming mugs of billy tea beside them. There was comparative silence till the meal was over, and then cigarettes were produced. Someone started to sing 'Waltzing Matilda', followed by 'Tie me kangaroo down, sport' and 'Salute Australia Fair'. Melissa's soprano rose high above the voices of the men, and Susan joined in with the bits she knew. It was all just how she had imagined it would be, and she wished that she could have stayed with the camp for another day, but with school awaiting her it was not possible. Melissa slipped away from the camp fire after a while, and Susan noted that Milton was also missing. Only the stockmen were left and presently Susan rose and said goodnight. Ian strolled with her to the tent.

"Have you enjoyed your day's mustering?" he asked, looking down into her shadowy face.

Susan laughed. "I can't really claim to have done

any mustering," she said, "but I've loved being a passenger."

"Shame you've got to go back to-morrow," he said. "Sue, d'you think—" He paused and came a step nearer to her, but just at. that moment there was a movement from the back of the tent, and Melissa appeared.

"Oh, hello," she said, plainly taken aback. "Just off to bed? So am I. G'night, Ian."

"Where have you been?" he asked, but Melissa had disappeared through the tent flap.

Susan looked at Ian and hesitated. What had he been about to say when interrupted by his sister? She waited, then turned impatiently away.

"Goodnight, Ian," she said. "See you in the morning."

The next morning early Ian took the two girls back to the homestead. Before starting back to the camp he said to Susan,

"Come and have a look at the cattle which have been mustered so far." She followed him on to the veranda, and looked out to where he was pointing. At first there seemed to be nothing but a vague cloud of dust. Then she saw them slowly approaching; cattle, and nothing but cattle, all crowding into the paddocks, rank upon rank of ever-moving horns and twitching tails. And now, as they left the natural screen of the hills and boulders behind them, the noise was becoming louder and louder. Susan could get glimpses of the dogs, too, ever watchful and ready to dart at the heels of any animal which showed signs of wandering. The bright shirts of the stockmen showed up as vivid patches of colour among the dun-coloured and the dust.

"My, oh, my!" Susan said softly. "I never imagined anything like this. How many are there, Ian?"

He laughed. "A few thousand; and these are not all by any means. We shall be mustering for weeks yet."

"Then what?"

He looked at the bright interested face raised to his. "Well, then we drive them down to the drifting yard where the prime beeves are put into the cattle train, liners they call them. They're taken to the cattle market at Mount Isa. The rest are sorted out for breeding purposes, and the young ones, the calves, are branded."

"How do such an enormous number of cattle get enough water to drink?" Susan asked. "What I mean is, even at the homestead with those three enormous tanks everyone has to be careful of water, so—?" she looked at him and waited.

Ian nodded, then pointed to a spot beyond the road and at the edge of the foothills.

"See that tall pylon," he said, "right out there on its own? Well, that's an artesian well, or bore as they are called. That's one of ours, but the Government have had bores sunk at various distances, for the cattle and sheep stations. The animals themselves are very clever at finding water if there happens to be any around. Here in the interior there's nearly always a shortage of water. Plenty during the wet, sometimes too much, but as soon as the season is over, the sun soon dries up the moisture. But you know, there's plenty of water underground, and these bores pump it up and direct it into channels and tanks. It's not nearly such a problem as it used to be before the Government took over."

Susan looked again at the distant scene; at the herds of animals still moving down towards the paddocks and thought that she would never forget this typical scene of pastoral Australia. She looked at Ian and saw that he was watching her.

"I shall be leaving for the camp very early in the morning," he said. "I—er—won't be seeing you till next weekend, I guess." And then suddenly, to Susan's astonishment, he lunged forward and kissed her awkwardly on the cheek. "Goodnight, Sue, till next weekend," and, before she could say anything in return he had gone.

But Ian did not see Susan the following weekend, and neither did she see him; for on the Thursday a message came over the air for her telling her that the Flying Doctor plane, a Cessna, was calling at the Homestead on Friday evening to pick her up and take her to Alice Springs. When Susan told Mrs McQuarrie of the message she said,

"Oh, that's fine, Sue; you'll be there in no time at all."

"But what about Ian?" Susan asked anxiously. "He'll be expecting—"

"Oh, he'll be coming home anyway for supplies, so don't worry about that."

Secretly Susan was disappointed, but she said no more on the subject.

The next day was crammed full of interest and stimulation for Susan. This was her first trip in a small private plane, and as the little machine skimmed along her eyes were everywhere—on the stretches of red earth, the glimpses of forest, and once the gleam of a small sheet of water. They passed above masses of grey and purple rocks and boulders, the ribbon of a bitumen road and the occasional swiftly-vanishing township. Susan felt suddenly that she was in a dream world and would wake up in Croydon any moment. When at last the plane touched down at Alice Springs airport, a pretty fair-haired young woman came forward to meet her. . .

"Hello," she said. "Miss Manley? I'm Mary Ferguson—I guess you know my voice anyway." Susan smiled and held out her hand. "This is my husband, Robin," Mrs Ferguson continued, turning to a pleasant-faced young man who was standing just behind her. Susan shook hands with him, and then the three of them moved over towards a parked car. During the drive into the town Mary Ferguson told Susan that her husband, Robin, was a doctor at the R.F.D. Base hospital.

"Really?" said Susan. "Oh, that's very interesting. I was hoping I'd meet someone who could tell me all about them."

"Oh, he'll do all that," Mary replied with a laugh. "Look, this is our main street—er—d'you mind if I call you Susan?"

"Of course not, please do." Susan was staring about her in dismay and disappointment. This was not what she had imagined the town of Alice Springs to be like; full of up-to-date shops, hotels and super-markets.

"You're disappointed and disillusioned, aren't you?" Mary Ferguson had been watching Susan's expressive face. "But wait. This is the modern part of the town. You'll see the old Alice later on."

"Mary," Robin called over his shoulder to his wife, "what about showing Susan our top-class hotel, the one where the Queen stayed?"

Mary laughed and looked at Susan. "Yes, it's where Queen Elizabeth slept," she said. "Just like some of your show-places in England, the only difference being that ours is Queen Elizabeth the second, while yours is Queen Elizabeth the first—or so I've heard!"

Robin stopped the car in front of a very smart modern hotel. There was a wide paved courtyard leading up to a flight of steps and wide swing doors. Inside the thickly carpeted foyer was delightfully cool and dim with venetian blinds at the windows. Robin led the two girls into the lounge and ordered drinks. Susan looked about her. The events of the day had so stimulated and excited her that now she was beginning to feel tired. There were not many people in the lounge, but as her eyes turned towards the door the figure of a man appeared. He was calling something over his shoulder to an unseen person behind him and Susan thought suddenly that there was something vaguely familiar about him. Then as he turned his head she saw to her amazement that it was Alan McQuarrie. He recognised Susan at the same moment, and then for a split second the two stared at each other. Susan was the first to recover from this surprise meeting.

"Alan!" she called, and waved a hand to him. His face broke into a delighted grin, and he crossed the room in a few strides.

"Why, Sue," he said, "what a delightful surprise! How come?" Mary and Robin were looking on with interest, and Susan hastened to make the introductions.

"Meet Alan McQuarrie," she said to them. "And,

Alan, this is Mary Ferguson, and her husband Robin.
I'm staying with them for the weekend."

"Sit down and join us in a drink," Robin invited
at once. He turned and gestured to the waiter.
"What's it to be?"

Alan sat down next to Susan. "Thanks, I'll have
a beer," he said, then looked again at Susan. She
smiled and realised that her feeling of tiredness had
quite vanished.

"I'm here just for the weekend to discuss plans
for the school's big party of the year" she said, and
Alan nodded and grinned.

"Of course; I should have remembered from my
own schooldays," he said. "Well, well—" he turned
and smiled into her face, and Susan noticed for the
second time how striking were the clear pale grey
eyes set in their heavy dark lashes. "It's good to see
you again, Sue."

She felt her cheeks warming under his gaze.

"But what are you doing here?" Then she turned
to Robin and Mary. "Alan is the son of the kind
people with whom I'm living," she said. "He's just
completed all his medical exams, and—" she glanced
enquiringly at Alan, "have you started on a—job
yet?"

"Yes—" he said after a pause. "But not as a
doctor—not yet. I've applied for the sort of job I
want, and in the meantime I've just started working
as a relief pilot at the R.F.D.S. Base."

The three others stared at him and then all started
to laugh.

"But that's where Robin is!" Mary explained to
the puzzled Alan. "He's on the staff of the base
hospital."

"Really?" Alan said eagerly, turning to Robin. "Well, you're just the chap I'd like to have a talk with. You see, the job I'm after is with the Flying Doctor Service. I came here only yesterday, having got this relief pilot job so that I could find out as much as possible of the practical side. D'you think—"

"Of course," Robin interrupted heartily, "I'll tell you everything you want to know, *and* show you round."

"Alan, what luck meeting like this!" Susan exclaimed.

"How about coming back to have a meal with us?" Robin suggested, then laughed. "Tell you what. *We* can talk flying doctors while the girls talk school get-togethers, and in that way everyone will be happy!"

And that was just how the evening was spent. Susan was rather disappointed that as the hours went by Alan did not show any desire to talk to her alone, or to ask for news of his family. 'Though I guess there's no reason why he should, things being as they are,' her thoughts ran, 'but still it would have been nice to hear the ins and outs of his news.' She listened to Mary Ferguson as the latter told her of the arrangements which had been made for the big get-together, and presently the two men joined in.

"Robin and I are taking you out to-morrow to see the site," Mary said to Susan. "And here is—" she produced from its folder a large closely-typed official-looking document, "the detailed plan of events. The underlying idea," Mary continued, "is not just entertainment in the ordinary sense; it's more psychological. You see, the hundreds of children who converge here for this yearly meeting are children who for the rest of the year never see any others but the few they meet for school every day, which makes them very limited. Even with a group of only four or five, one is by nature the leader. You agree?" Susan nodded, thinking of Martin Gregson in her own little school. "Well now, that leader," Mary went on, "could be a good leader, or on the other hand, could be a bully. Now, by coming here and taking part in sports and contests of all kinds with hundreds of other boys and girls, that leader finds his own level, his true level, sometimes quite painfully, too. For of course there are fights, bound to be. But I've never yet known a child who didn't want to come back again and again, though unfortunately it's not always possible."

Susan nodded again. "Yes," she agreed, "I can see now how important this is."

"Then there's the loneliness of the outback," Mary continued. "It breeds shyness in the kids, and the grown-ups too. Sometimes when the children first come here they're quite tongue-tied with shyness." She laughed. "But it soon wears off, I can tell you! This annual party really does do a great deal of good. It brings new interest and stimulation into lives which are of necessity very narrow. What's your little lot like?"

But before Susan could give an answer Robin jumped to his feet.

"Come on, get off your hobby-horse, love," he said to his wife. "I could do with a cuppa."

"Sorry," said Mary, and went off to make the inevitable pot of tea. Soon after this Alan rose to go. Mary and Robin said goodnight, and Susan walked with Alan down the veranda steps and to the garden gate. Susan was the first to speak.

"Alan, when are you coming home again?" she asked.

He glanced at her, then laughed shortly.

"Home?" he said. "Well, I don't really know. Could be any time. There are various things I ought to pack to take with me, so I shall have to manage another trip soon."

"What made you think of joining the Flying Doctors?" Susan asked next. It was a question she had wanted to put to him all evening but had not had a chance. Alan glanced sideways at her, then took her arm as they reached the gate.

"Why not?" he asked, turning to face her. "I don't want to settle down—well, not just yet, and there are endless opportunities for moving around in the R.F.D.S." He laughed "Wouldn't it attract you if you were a chap and in my shoes? After all, Sue, you must be pretty adventurous yourself."

She laughed and knew that he was right.

"Yes, I think it would," she said. "It must be a wonderful life." Then, as he turned from her to open the gate, she added, "Alan, how come you're a pilot? I've been wanting to ask you all evening."

He laughed again and squeezed her arm. "Oh, I got my pilot's licence some years ago when I was at home. That was when we had our own plane. Then—" his eyes crinkled in sudden laughter, "one day I pranged the machine and the boss swore he'd never have another; and he never has. Ian's not keen on flying, anyway."

"Oh!" Susan laughed with him. "I've thought several times that there must have been a plane there once; you know, with the air-strip, and the hangar still there."

"Yes—well, you know what the Old Man's like—mind as immovable as a block of concrete." There was a short pause, then Alan said rather abruptly,

"Look, Ssuan, what about—er—doing something together to-morrow? You'll be returning in the evening, I suppose."

Susan nodded, with a pleasant sense of anticipation. Yes, it would certainly be interesting to go out to-morrow with Alan, just the two of them. Perhaps he would tell her about this mysterious rift with his family. But perhaps not; and in any case it did not matter whether he did or not. She would still like to go out in his company.

"Yes," she said, smiling at him, "I'd love to."

"Well now, I'm on duty all morning at the hospital," Alan said. "What about—would two-thirty suit you? I thought you might like to see the John Flynn Memorial Church, and the museum. I hope that doesn't sound too stuffy. Perhaps you—"

"Oh, but that sounds fine," smiled Susan. "I can't think of anything I'd rather do and see."

"Good. Well—" He looked at her, hesitated for a moment, then smiled and put a hand on her shoulder. "Well—" he said again, "er—goodnight, Sue; see you to-morrow."

Susan lingered there at the gate till she heard the sound of his car starting up, then she turned and strolled thoughtfully back to the house. 'Alan seems a different person,' she thought, 'away from his home and family. He's really nice, not a bit rude, and rather shy.'

Sunday morning was full of interest for Susan. To begin with Robin and Mary took her in the car to see the studio from which the lessons for the School of the Air were broadcast. It was just a large room with a table and a chair. On the table was the transceiver and beside them was the piano. Susan stared round at the empty room; a classroom, but with no desks, chairs or children, 'And yet,' she suddenly thought with a feeling almost of awe, 'this is one of the biggest classrooms in the world.' It must be, for its pupils, hundreds of them, were spread out across thousands of miles. Over mountains, forests and deserts. All their voices were collected in this one room. She looked at Mary and the latter smiled, and nodded in unspoken agreement.

The next port of call was the camping ground, and it was on the way there that Susan really got the feel of the old frontier town of Alice Springs, the desert town right in the centre of this vast continent. Here were the narrow dusty tracks, the lonely clumps of ghost gums, the occasional tortured-looking skeletons of trees, the red earth and burnt grass stretching for flat mile upon mile to the far horizon. And the silence was everywhere. The sports arena and the camping site were some miles distant, but the land was so flat that it could easily be seen. The huge shed with its tin roof dominated the scene. As the car drew nearer Susan could see that the sports ground itself was surrounded by a fence. Beside the big shed were ablution huts and beyond them she could see the silvery shine of water tanks.

"Nothing much to see at present," Mary told her, as the car came to a standstill, "but wait till the big day. Hundreds of tents all in rows, more rows of parked cars and vans, and, last but not least, masses of milling kids." She raised her hands, then let them fall in a gesture of exhaustion. "Gosh, when I think of it——" She paused, then burst out laughing. "But it's fun all the same!"

"I can hardly wait," Susan said, grinning.

Robin glanced at his watch.

"Better be getting back, dear," he said to his wife. "I'm on duty this afternoon, you know."

Promptly at two-thirty Alan arrived in his little car. Susan watched him come up the path of the Ferguson bungalow. The bright sun beat down upon his thick, neutral-tinted hair and his narrowed grey eyes glinted from between the thick dark lashes. He smiled and waved to Susan, and she walked down the steps to meet him.

"Hello there," he said. "You're looking as beautiful as the morning. Ready?"

"Wouldn't you like a cold drink before we start?" Susan asked, but he shook his head.

"Don't tempt me; if I sat down on that shady veranda I wouldn't want to get up. Let's get going right away. The light's just right for the church; it's rather special, you know."

"Oh," said Susan, as he helped her into the car, "in what way is it special?"

"You just wait and see." He smiled at her, then started the engine. She looked sideways at his face, and could hardly believe that this was the same disgruntled, embittered young man who had arrived so suddenly at Kanoch Doon; and yet this was the real Alan, Susan felt sure. What had happened to him, and his family, to have brought about such an unhappy situation? Whose fault was it? For Alan's parents were honest, straightforward, and very likeable, as was Ian, the elder brother. What had happened, back there in the past? Susan wondered, then gave it up in her enjoyment of the present. The car had turned off the bitumen road on to a narrow track. She could see the church in the distance, and presently they stopped in front of it. Susan studied it with interest, for it was like no other church she had seen, either in England or in Adelaide. It was very plain, with no columns, spires or steeples. Her first impression was of white and red stone. In front of the building was a half-circular courtyard with wide open plate glass doors at the far end. The courtyard itself was paved with irregular-shaped stones, coloured red. Alan alighted from the car and helped Susan out, and they walked side by side into the courtyard.

"This is sandstone," Alan said, looking down at the flagstones. "Notice the five windows up there, Susan?" and he pointed to the front of the church. She looked and saw that above the entrance were five rose-coloured marble panels, and set in each was a grilled window of gleaming white porcelain. "They're the equivalent of the usual stained glass windows in the old traditional style," he went on, taking Susan's arm and leading her forward. "But they serve a double purpose, for they're ventilators as well." They had reached the entrance by now and he led the way in. It was refreshingly cool inside and Susan at once noticed a very significant thing. Instead of the semi-gloom to which she was accustomed in most churches, in this one there was clear gleaming light everywhere. Alan was watching her face and then he nodded towards the sanctuary. She looked and then saw what he meant. The walls were of glass, the continuity broken only by marble columns of palest pink. The effect was almost unearthly in its beauty.

"Oh, it's lovely!" she murmured softly, and Alan smiled. They moved slowly forward towards what looked like a glowing red wall of sandstone in the shape of a shield. In the centre, and seeming to stand out with a kind of haloed light, was the cross. Susan stared and realised that this halo was the sunlight fretted through the massive masonry from outside. She looked slowly around and was all at once conscious of a feeling of emptiness and space, and then she saw that there were no plaques or brass plates anywhere in this church.

"D'you get the feeling?" Alan asked in a subdued voice. "The feeling of being actually out—in the bush, all alone?" She nodded, and he pointed to the tall nave windows, and through them Susan saw the red earth and the dried-up bush stretching away as far as she could see. "That was what John Flynn saw—most of his life," Alan added. They moved slowly back up the aisle, and out again into the courtyard.

"Come and I'll show you the Pioneers' Wall," Alan said. He took Susan's hand lightly in his and led her to another courtyard which enclosed the Shrine Circle on the southern side of the church. "Here are laid the ashes of Flynn's friends of the Outback—all the people who helped him in his work, in however small and humble a way." He pointed and Susan saw rows and rows of bronze plaques let into the wall, giving the names and details of each.

Encircling the church and its environs was a Garden of Remembrance, bright with the purple of bougainvillea, and the yellow of wattle, as well as many garden flowers which Susan recognised. As she walked out into the bright sunlight beside Alan she gazed back over her shoulder and said softly,

"That was a wonderful experience, Alan. What a beautiful church! It must be quite unique."

"Well, not exactly," he said, leading her towards the car. "Not architecturally, that is. There are several churches built in this plain, sweeping up to the sky, kind of style; they're all in the north, though. There's one at Darwin, in the new country which is gradually being opened up. D'you like the style?"

"Yes, I do, definitely. They just suit the country; the open, thrusting, pioneering sort of land. I find it all terribly stimulating. Where's the museum, Alan?"

He was still holding her hand, and now he led her away from the car.

"Well, I almost forgot the museum," he said, "but it's right here," and he led her towards the corner of the building. "It's at the western side of the church. Here we are." They passed through the entrance doors and Alan released Susan's hand. She looked about her. It was quite a small room, and almost the first thing she saw was an old pedal generator set. Mounted just above it, and in the actual operating position, was the 'Number One Transceiver'. Close by Susan saw an old Morse-sending keyboard.

"Is the Morse keyboard still used?" she asked Alan as they examined it together.

"No, not any more. It was followed up quite soon by the development of voice transmission, and," he smiled at her, "you know all about that, of course. Come over here and look at this; it's the centrepiece of the museum." Susan followed him to where a scale model of the biplane 'Victory' was displayed.

"It's the first plane which was used by the Flying Doctor Service at Cloncurry."

Susan examined the model, then looked at the walls of the room which were partially covered by small maps and charts.

"What are all these?" she asked, going over to them.

Alan followed. "They're maps of the district, some only half-prepared, as you can see, but they show what he had in mind, the scope and immensity of the project, once he'd got it going. He was a wonderful man. Over here now——" he moved on a few paces and Susan followed him to a large show-case——"are some of Flynn's personal belongings. Here is his academic 'hood' as it was then called. There——" he pointed, "is the blackened old billycan that brewed the tea he loved to share with the simple folk he met everywhere on his journeyings through the dry and dusty inland. Over here——" he, strolled on a few paces, "is a picture of the old horse-drawn buckboard he used so often, and here——" he moved on again and pointed, "is a picture of John Flynn himself."

Susan moved up after him and studied the face of the man in the picture.

"He looks a bit like you," she said.

Alan stared, then laughed.

"That's the finest compliment you could pay me," he said, and turned towards the door. "Well, that's that, I'm afraid. Enjoyed it, Sue?"

"Yes, very much," she smiled, and again she marvelled at the change in him. 'Alan's certainly a young man of surprises,' she thought.

"The next item on the agenda is a nice long cool drink," Alan said. "How about it?"

It was while Susan was thoroughly enjoying an iced orange squash in the hotel lounge that Alan turned to her and said,

"When is this big get-together of yours, Sue, and how long does it last? I seem to remember from my own not so distant youth that it went on for nearly a week."

"No, just a long week-end really, from Friday to Tuesday. The date hasn't yet been fixed. Mary hasn't mentioned it, but I do know that it will be within the next month." She paused for a moment, then asked, "Will you still be here then?"

"Shouldn't think so, but—" he hesitated as if about to say more, then seemed to change his mind. "Well, it's been nice meeting up with you again." His voice sounded very formal all at once, and Susan wondered why. Had she said anything to offend him?

"It's been nice for me, too," she said. "It was a lovely surprise."

There was a brief silence between them, and then Alan glanced at his watch.

"I must be getting back to the hospital," he said. "I'm on call from seven, so—"

"Then I mustn't keep you," Susan said quickly, as she rose to her feet. "Let's go." Quite suddenly the friendly feeling between them seemed to have vanished, and she wondered again why. Perhaps she had expected too much.

On the way back to the Fergusons' bungalow Alan chatted about trivial things, but just before he left her at the gate Susan looked at him and said in a rather uncertain tone of voice,

"Any messages for home, Alan?"

He stared straight in front of him for a short while, then shook his head.

"Not even for your mother?" she asked with a sudden surge of anger for his obstinacy. "Surely you have a message for *her*. How can I tell them I met you without—"

"Then don't," he cut in roughly, but added almost at once, "Sorry. Yes, all right, give my love to Ma and Melissa, but don't say anything about—my plans for the future. Tell them I'll write." He stopped abruptly and looked at her. "Hasn't Ian said—anything to you about me?"

"No, of course not." Susan's voice was quite indignant. "It's really none of my business, but—" she hesitated, then added, "well, you're all so nice that I do wish you would—sort it all out and then everyone would be happy again."

Alan laughed shortly. "Oh, yeah?" he said, and raised an eyebrow at her. "Well, well, as you said yourself, it's no business of yours; and I'd hate to bore you with the story of why I've quarrelled with my family. If you want to know ask brother Ian."

"As if I would!" Susan almost snapped at him. "I just wish that it could be settled and cleared up. It's such a senseless way of going on, and—" she hesitated, and Alan glanced down at her flushed face; glanced down only slightly, for she was almost as tall as he; then he leant forward and drew his finger along the curve of her cheek.

"You're very sweet, Sue," he said. "Brother Ian's a lucky chap," and with a nod and a grin he was off.

Susan stared after him for a surprised moment, then started after him.

"Alan!" she called urgently, but he was already out

of earshot, and presently she heard the sound of the car engine starting up.

'Oh, what an idiot he is!' she thought crossly. 'Why *do* people jump to conclusions? Well, I'll have to think of a way now of letting him know that he's on the wrong tack entirely, but—well, is he?' she suddenly asked herself. 'Ian is very nice, you like him, quite a lot, *and* he is attracted to you, you know that. Well then?' But mentally she shrugged her shoulders and knew that she was not yet ready to answer that question. All she was certain of at present was that she had an interesting and satisfying job, and she did not want to become involved with anything else—not just yet.

CHAPTER 5

SUSAN arrived back at Kanoch Doon late on Sunday evening. Ian and Melissa came down to the small air-strip to meet her. Ian picked up her small case and as the three of them walked up to the homestead Susan saw that there were several long cattle trains drawn up beside the paddocks.

"Well," said Ian, smiling down at her, "had a good weekend, Sue?"

"Yes, marvellous. I see the mustering's still going merrily on."

Mrs McQuarrie appeared on the veranda. "Ah, there you are!" she called. "Good to see you back, lass. Come along in."

"I'm off for a shower," said Ian. "I'll put your case in your room, Sue. All the news later." Melissa also disappeared and Susan followed Mrs McQuarrie into the kitchen.

"Gosh, something smells good," she smiled.

"Yes, you're just in time. I've been baking splits. Sit down and have some while I pour you a cup of tea."

"How's everything here?" Susan asked, tucking into the split which Mrs McQuarrie had filled generously with jam and thick cream.

"Oh, all right, you know. Mustering's still going on, and Ian and the boss go back to the camp early to-morrow, but it won't be much longer now." She paused. "See anyone you knew at the Alice?"

Susan looked at her in surprise. 'She must know that Alan's there,' she thought, and took a drink of tea.

"Well, yes, I did," she said. "I saw Alan—and he sent his love to you."

Mrs McQuarrie paused in the act of filling another split.

"Alan?" she repeated, and stared at Susan. "So he is there! How—was he looking, and—?" she stopped abruptly.

Susan waited for a second, then said quickly, "He's looking very well indeed. He took me to see the John Flynn Memorial Church, and he—told me to tell you that he'll be writing soon."

Mrs McQuarrie nodded slowly, then said, "Well, I'm glad of that. I'll tell Douglas; he'll be glad to hear." She glanced again at Susan, who was now busily getting through her second split, seemed about to say something more, then silently turned back to the oven.

Susan said no more, and presently rose and made her way back to her own room where she had a shower and changed into fresh clothing. Then she unpacked her case and strolled back to the front veranda. Everyone was gathered there as usual. Ian came and sat beside Susan, and then Melissa joined them and began to ask eager questions about the Alice.

The evening followed its usual pattern of talk, light refreshments and some music, and Susan felt pleasantly at home again. Douglas McQuarrie went off early to bed, and Susan thought that his wife looked rather worried as she followed him in a few minutes.

"The boss hasn't been too good lately," Ian confided to Susan when she looked at him enquiringly. "He never lets up, you know, and of course he's not getting any younger. However, the biggest part of the mustering is over, thank goodness."

Susan herself was beginning to feel tired after her long day and was suddenly overcome by a huge yawn.

"Sorry, Ian," she said, and got to her feet. "I'm terribly sleepy. D'you mind if I—" but he rose with her, then, somewhat to her surprise, took her arm and walked with her to her own room. As they walked down the veranda steps she was conscious of Melissa's teasing smile.

"So you really enjoyed your weekend at the Alice?" Ian asked, looking down into her face. "I—er—suppose it must seem rather dull and quiet back here in Kangaroo."

Susan stared, then started to laugh.

"What's the joke?" Ian enquired.

"Nothing, really; it's just that that's the first time I've ever heard you call your home Kangaroo. I've heard it from the children, and occasionally from Melissa, but—"

"Yes, I know," he interrupted a trifle impatiently. "I don't like it, but sometimes it slips out. It's the abos' interpretation of Kanoch Doon, as I expect you've heard. The boss loathes the name, but—well, there it is. Anyway, *do* you find it dull and quiet here?"

Susan looked at him; they had reached her own veranda now and she paused for a moment.

"No, of course I don't," she said at last. "Otherwise I wouldn't still be here—would I?" But before Ian could reply to Susan's question she had run lightly up the veranda steps and into her room. "Goodnight, Ian," came her voice through the darkness. "Till tomorrow!"

Life at Kanoch Doon slipped into its familiar pleasant routine for Susan, and presently the mustering was over and the men were back on the station. Susan's pupils were very interested in her account of her weekend in Alice Springs, and of course the date of the get-together.

"I don't know," she told them, "but it will be some time soon, and in the meantime you must settle down and do your lessons. Understand?"

Everyone at the homestead was now eager to know the date of the big schools' party. In fact it became the topic of the moment.

"You'll find that most of the kids' parents will be there," Mrs McQuarrie told Susan one afternoon after school had been dismissed. "I used to go in the old days."

There was a clatter on the veranda and Ian came in.

"Am I hungry?" he grinned, and sniffed. "What about—" He smiled across at Susan.

"It's all ready," his mother told him. "I was just waiting for your father. Where's Melissa?"

"Need you ask? Out in the far paddock, of course. She'll never make a teacher's training college, Ma, but I think if you substitute agricultural training for teacher's training it'll suit my little sister much better." He moved across to Susan's side.

Mrs McQuarrie looked at him in a worried fashion.

"And yet she did so well at school," she said. "All

those 'A' levels or whatever it is that they call them. Your father and I both thought—"

"Yes, Ma, I know," Ian interrupted, "but it's no good you and the boss trying to force the kid into something she doesn't want."

"No question of forcing," his mother said testily. "She wanted it in the beginning—or so she said."

"At seventeen you can't be expected to know your own mind for two minutes together. You'd better have a talk with her. Well, I must be getting back. See you later, Sue."

Susan wandered back to her room. She corrected some of the children's exercises, then had her usual shower and changed into a gay red and white checked frock. Ian had said nothing about a ride or a walk for the evening, but he might get round to it later. However, after the six o'clock meal everyone gathered as usual on the front veranda. Susan thought Melissa was looking scared and yet excited at the same time. 'I wonder if they've all had their talk,' she thought, and looked at Ian. And it was while she was trying to puzzle out the expression on his face that they all heard the rather unusual sound of an approaching plane; rather unusual for the time of day. They stared at each other in turn, then Mr McQuarrie turned to Ian and said,

"We're not expecting anyone from town, are we?"

"Not that I know of."

The two men rose and went off in the direction of the landing strip at the back of the homestead.

"Maybe it's the flying doctor," said Melissa, rising in her turn. "He may have been paying a visit to one of the out-stations and thought he'd drop in here for a drink. I hope so. Coming, Susan?"

The two girls hurried off after Ian and his father, and Susan was filled with a pleasant sense of anticipation. 'What fun if it's Robin from Alice Springs,' she thought; or even—well, it could be Alan, too, piloting the plane. She hurried after Melissa, and they joined Ian and his father at the dusty home-made air strip. Susan watched the small plane as it approached, circled, then prepared to come down. Suddenly Melissa started to jig up and down with excitement.

"It's Alan!" she exclaimed, grabbing Susan's arm. "Look, there he is, he's waving!"

Susan stared, but the plane had turned and was now gliding towards them along the strip. It came to a halt, the door opened, and out climbed Robin, followed more slowly by Alan. Melissa ran forward, then Ian and his father advanced to meet the newcomers. Susan followed and waved to the two. She gave a quick glance at Mr McQuarrie as he greeted his younger son. Robin turned to Susan.

"I've got a message for you from Mary," he said, but the boss cut in with,

"That'll wait for a minute or two. Come on up to the house and rinse the dust out of your throats. Well, how's things, Alan?" His voice sounded normal, but Susan saw that his face set in hard lines.

Alan's face was pale as he replied to his father, but then he turned and smiled at Susan as the whole party moved slowly towards the house.

"Well, this is very welcome," Robin said a few seconds later as he sat on the shady veranda drinking something long and cool. "I expect you're all wondering what we're doing here. Well, I had to visit a patient out this way, and as I knew we'd be almost passing over Alan's home, I asked specially for him to be my pilot, and at the same time brought a message for you, Susan." He fumbled in his pocket and produced a letter. "Incidentally, Mary still talks about that pleasant foursome we had with you and Alan. We must do it again some time."

"Thanks, Robin," Susan said, as she took the letter from him, wondering at the same time what part Alan had played in this arrangement; or had it been just sprung on him? She glanced quickly at him and met the direct impact of his clear light eyes. He smiled at her and it seemed to Susan that there was an unspoken question in them. She felt the colour warming her cheeks and involuntarily looked at Ian, but he was staring straight in front of him.

Quite soon Robin rose to his feet and then everyone trooped back to the air-strip to see them off. Mrs McQuarrie had been very quiet all this time, but Susan noticed that she was clinging to Alan's arm. Goodbyes were called, and then just before he climbed into the cockpit, Susan found Alan beside her. His hand touched hers very lightly as he murmured in her ear, "Be seeing you soon again at the Alice, Sue."

Susan's heart gave a quick little jump at these words, and at that moment, and as she smiled into Alan's face, her eyes seemed to be drawn to one side and she saw that Ian was watching her. She felt slightly uncomfortable under the steady glance of his blue eyes, but then came the feeling of impatience. Why should she feel like this? Alan's words were perfectly ordinary, and of course she would almost certainly see him when she went again to Alice Springs, but—and here her heart seemed to miss a beat as she suddenly recalled Robin's words as he had handed her his wife's letter. 'That pleasant foursome with you and Alan,' he had said, and 'We must do it again some time.' Of course, Ian must be wondering why she had never mentioned seeing Alan, and equally of course the reason was quite simple. Alan had asked her not to. But Ian did not know this. Now what would he make of it all? Susan wondered rather unhappily.

She looked again at Ian, but he was talking to his mother and they were turning to walk back to the house. Susan called a goodnight to them and took Mary's letter to her own room to read. 'I must think of a way to clear up any misunderstanding,' she thought as she ripped open the letter and began to read. As she had expected it gave the date for the get-together, just two weeks hence, and the itinerary; also leaflets to be distributed among the children for the parents' information. The letter went on to say, 'Robin will be able to give you this in person, and he was also able to arrange for your friend Alan to be his pilot, which must have been a pleasant surprise to him when he told Alan that he would be able to pay his folks a quick visit. I must say Alan seemed quite overcome. I hope it will be a pleasant surprise to you too, my dear.'

Susan had a quick feeling of annoyance, for she thought she detected an arch note in the last few words of the letter. 'What an awful lot of match-makers these people of the Outback are!' she thought. 'First, there's Alan, who seemed to think that Ian and I—and now here's Mary Ferguson with ideas about Alan and me; and now I suppose Ian will be wondering about me too. What a mix-up! However,' she looked thoughtful for a moment, 'it's evident that Alan had nothing to do with this visit.'

The next morning when Susan gave her news to the children the excitement was intense and she was hard put to it to maintain even a semblance of order. At last she decided in desperation to read the riot act.

"Now listen, children," she called, her voice rising above the clamour, "unless this noise stops at once, and everyone gets on with the exercises set, I shall write to Alice Springs and tell them that *this* school will *not* be attending the get-together because—" she paused, and the children stared at her with round shocked eyes—"they don't know how to behave."

There was an uneasy silence; then Mary said,

"Oh, Miss Susan, you—you wouldn't do that, would you?"

"Not unless I have to," Susan said, steeling herself against the imploring eyes raised to hers. "But you know what to do about it, don't you?"

The children nodded and there was an almost uncanny silence for the rest of the morning.

Susan gave her news to the family when they were all gathered on the veranda after tea. Melissa's eyes lighted up with excitement.

"I'll be coming with you, Susan," she said, and then turned to her brother. "You'll take us in, Ian, won't you?"

Susan thought he hesitated for a moment before nodding to his sister. "And there's the dance at Eighty-Mile," Melissa continued. "It's on Saturday." She looked again at her brother, then at Susan.

"You'd like to go, Susan, wouldn't you, lass?" Mrs McQuarrie cut in unexpectedly. "You'll take them along, Ian, won't you?"

Susan did not look at him; she was feeling distinctly uncomfortable.

"I don't mind at all," she said at last, "one way or the other."

"Of course we'll go," Ian said abruptly. "Why not?"

Susan looked at him and felt she could have slapped or even kicked him with the greatest of pleasure. He hardly looked at her for the rest of the evening and she was glad when it came to an end and she could go off to her own room. She hoped now that Melissa would change her mind about this dance, though it did occur to her that the evening might provide an opportunity for clearing up the situation which had arisen between herself and Ian.

However, when Susan met him the next day he was his usual cheerful self again and referred quite happily to the coming dance. Susan wondered hopefully if he would suggest one of their evening rides before then, but he did not. And as the days passed she thought she noticed Mrs McQuarrie observing them both with thoughtful eyes. Melissa also seemed to have noticed the slackening off in her brother's interest in Susan, for one evening while the two girls were together in the garden she suddenly said,

"What's wrong with you and Ian? Haven't quarrelled, have you?"

Susan could feel her cheeks flushing under the other girl's eye.

"No, of course not," she said. "What would we have to quarrel about?"

"Well, I wouldn't know." Melissa paused, then added, "Haven't fallen for Alan by any chance, have you?"

"Melissa, what things you do say!" Susan's eyes were beginning to snap as she turned on the younger girl. "You really are the limit—and it's no business of yours anyway."

"No—but you haven't answered my question."

"And I don't intend to; it's too ridiculous anyway."

"Oh, well," Melissa said airily, "I hope you settle on *one* of my brothers. It's quite time they got married, and—I like you."

Susan turned to look at her, and then they both burst out laughing.

Susan found that Milton was making up the fourth for the dance and on Saturday evening the four of them set off in the utility. When they arrived at the hotel Ian suggested that they should go into the lounge first and all have a drink. Almost the first person they saw when they entered the big room was Letty French sitting at a table with another girl and two young men.

"Hi!" she called when she saw Ian, and then said something rapidly to the rest of her party. They all rose and came trooping over. "Hello, Melissa, Milton, what about joining up into one big party? Hello, Susan." She turned to the other girl with her and the two young men. "You've all met, I think. Bob—" to one of the party, "bring up some chairs."

"Oh, yes," said Melissa, her eyes dancing, "let's have a real bonzer party."

Susan sank into a chair feeling flat all at once. She had a sudden premonition that this was going to be anything but a bonzer party for her. She glanced at Letty and saw that she had seated herself beside Ian. He had called to the waiter and was ordering drinks.

"My, but it's weeks since I saw you all," Letty continued, her eyes on Ian's face.

'Since you saw Ian, you mean,' Susan thought, then turned to reply to something said by one of the young men. Melissa was chattering away to the other one, and Susan saw that Milton was beginning to look sulky. Presently Melissa and the young man got up and went off to dance. Letty turned to Ian, raising large eyes to his face,

"Dance with me, Ian," she said softly. "It's such ages since—" and she put a coaxing hand on his.

He looked at her and then at Susan.

"Well—" he began uncertainly, "perhaps—later on, Letty. You see—er—I brought Susan along, and I feel—"

"Oh, don't mind me," Susan said, suddenly irritated with him. "There's no need to feel duty-bound, Ian. You please yourself." She had no sooner spoken than she regretted her words, and as she just caught the half-smile on Letty's face, Susan knew that she had played straight into the other girl's hands. Ian rose without another word and drew Letty up with him. Milton looked at Susan.

"Dance?" he said, and she rose and followed him into the other room. "What the hell did that lot have to tack themselves on to us for?" he muttered in Susan's ear as they joined the other dancers. "I don't think Ian is too pleased."

"Well, he's trying hard," said Susan, catching a triumphant glance from Letty French as she and her partner swept past.

Milton grunted.

"Well, I must say you did your best to push him

into her eager arms," he commented. "Oh, hell, this is a real cow of a party!"

"You don't have to show your boredom and disappointment so plainly!" Susan snapped at him. "You did ask me to dance."

He stared at her in hurt surprise.

"I'm sorry," he muttered. "You know I didn't mean anything like that; but—well, I'd been looking forward to this evening, and now it's all gone wrong."

Susan felt repentant at once.

"Let's try and make it go right, then," she suggested. The music was slowing to a stop, and they returned to the other room. Melissa came up almost at the same moment. Susan nudged Milton and he slipped into the chair beside Melissa. Ian and Letty also appeared, Letty chattering brightly, one hand still on Ian's arm. She sat down and drew him down beside her, and Susan moved in determinedly on the other side. 'Not that I mind where he sits,' she was thinking, 'but Letty's not going to have it all her own way!'

Susan turned to speak to Ian, but found that he was replying to something Letty had said to him in a lowered tone of voice. At that moment the dance music came surging through the door once more and the young man Bob, who was on Susan's other side, asked her very politely to dance. She glanced once again at Ian, but his head was still turned in Letty's direction, so she rose and followed Bob out of the room. 'What an evening!' Susan thought as she circled the room in Bob's not very expert arms.

A little later on Ian did ask her to dance. Stiffly and silently she followed him towards the dance floor. They danced for a while in silence, then Ian said,

"I don't know why I come to dances. I don't—"

"So you're not enjoying it?" Susan interrupted.

"Oh I wouldn't say that. It's just that—I don't seem to get the hang of it. Oh, I'm enjoying the evening all right."

"Just sitting and talking, you mean?" Susan knew that she was behaving badly, but she did not seem able to help herself. Everything had gone wrong with this party right from the beginning, and now all she wanted was to get away and back to her own room. She had given up all hope now of being able to talk to Ian and to clear up the possible misunderstanding over Alan. Ian did not reply to her last remark, and soon after this, to almost everyone's relief, the party broke up. Goodbyes were said, and just as the utility was starting off, Letty called.

"I'll be out your way soon, Ian." Susan glanced sideways at him as he waved an acknowledgment. Melissa and Milton were very quiet on the way home, and Susan had an idea that they had quarrelled. Ian drove with a look of grim endurance on his face, while Susan sat in almost complete silence beside him.

CHAPTER 6

DURING the week that followed Susan made one or two efforts to break down the barrier that had arisen between herself and Ian, for she sincerely liked him and had enjoyed their friendship. But though he was pleasant as always Susan felt there was no real response. He never gave her an opportunity for a talk without others around, and after a few days she gave up trying. In any case there was so much to do in preparation for the big visit to Alice Springs that she literally had no time to give to personal problems.

Susan had had one moment when her hopes had risen high, and that was when Melissa had suddenly changed her mind about attending the get-together. Surely, she had thought, on that long whole-day drive to Alice Springs, she and Ian would be able to sort out their differences; but then she had learnt that as well as herself Ian was taking along a couple of the children with their parents. 'So that's that,' Susan thought dispiritedly.

Excitement among the children rose steadily till at last the day of departure arrived and off they all went in the utility with Ian driving. This journey by car to Alice Springs was very different from Susan's previous one, and as she stared about her she thought that it was very much more interesting and exciting. There was so much to see at close quarters. First there was the big black emu which suddenly appeared from behind a clump of twisted trees. It galloped along beside the car for several miles, then as if realising that the competition was unfair it stopped and gazed after them with puzzled eyes before turning on its tracks and disappearing behind a rampart of rocks. Then there was the hut, made from flattened tin cans, half hidden among the spinifex, and from which a blackfellow and his lubra emerged to wave at them. Their teeth flashed white as they grinned at the passing car, and Susan saw, with breathless interest, that the man was carrying a boomerang. In fact, there was so much to see that for Susan at least the time just flashed by. Lunch was taken in picnic style and sitting in the car for shade.

As they approached Alice Springs the semi-desert country gave place very gradually to stretches of almost green grass and mulga scrub with the occasional tall ragged eucalyptus. Ian pointed to one of which the bark was snow-white.

"That's a ghost gum," he told Susan in the impersonal voice he had been using to her of late. "Remind me to show you some pictures we have at home of these gums painted by the aboriginal artist, Albert Namatjiro."

"I'd love to see them," Susan replied, wishing that Ian did not sound so polite and distant, almost like a guide, she thought. Just then they passed a couple of aborigine drovers in wide felt hats and coloured shirts, and with the usual shaggy dogs, driving their cattle along in a dense cloud of dust. They waved and shouted as they passed.

As they came to the outskirts of the town the air was distinctly cooler and fresher. Everyone began to perk up, including the two children in the back of the car. Susan remarked on the change in the atmosphere, and Ian said,

"Yes, you see, it's nearly two thousand feet above sea level; makes a difference."

It seemed to Susan, looking about her, that they entered the town suburbs quite suddenly. One minute they were still out in the semi-desert, and the next the car was passing along a tidy fenced road with shady bungalows on either side. Through tall trees and flowering shrubs Susan could glimpse swimming pools and tennis courts. The most extravagantly-coloured sunset she had ever seen was splashing its reds, yellows and mauves over everything, and the general effect was of moving along in a prism of colour. There was, too, a buoyancy in the air, and, in spite of the bungalows and swimming pools, the exhilarating feel of a frontier town of the early years. Flocks of greyish-pink galahs and white cockatoos flew overhead, making for their roosting trees.

Ian drove along the wide main street, turned left at the bottom and headed for the camping site, and the scene when they got there made Susan gasp. Tents were everywhere, but in straight tidy lines; each line with the name and place from which the children came. Camp-fires were already being lighted and columns of blue smoke rose into the air. Dogs, attracted by the smell of cooking food, had managed to find their way in and were scampering about between the tents. Ian soon found the tents that had been allotted to Susan and her pupils, and after settling them in he led them to the camp-fire where they were to have their evening meal. There Susan met Mary Ferguson and some of the organisers and quite a number of parents from Kanoch Doon cattle station. Ian was to stay the night, and Susan was secretly glad about this. She hoped that later on, after the children were safely in bed, she would be able to have a few words with him in private and perhaps get back to their former friendly footing. Fortunately, the children were tired out, and after their meal were only too ready to be tucked in for the night.

Susan herself was feeling by this time that she would be heartily glad to call it a day, but she was determined to have her talk with Ian. 'It's such a marvellous opportunity,' she was thinking as, having said goodnight to her charges, she made her way back to the camp fire. However, on arrival she got the surprise of her life, for there, sitting beside Ian, was—Alan. She stopped and stared at him for a moment, not quite knowing whether to be pleased or not. Of course it was nice seeing Alan so soon, she thought, but what of her talk with Ian now?

"Hello, Sue," Alan said, rising to his feet and grinning at her impishly.

"Why—hello, Alan." She held out her hand. "I didn't—er—I wasn't expecting to see you—so soon," she finished hurriedly, and knowing that her words were ill-chosen.

His teeth gleamed in the half-darkness as he took her hand.

"Didn't you?" he said. "But I told you I'd be seeing you, didn't I? *My* surprise was seeing brother Ian here." He turned to face him. "Why, it must be years since you were here last."

"And you," Ian countered, and Susan sighed. 'Off they go again!' she thought. "I brought Susan and some of the children along," he added. "Now, what brought *you* here?" He stared into his brother's face and Alan stared back with a grin on his own.

"Why, just to look up old friends—and of course to see Susan again."

"Well, why don't we sit down?" Susan interrupted quickly. 'Anything to stop this verbal warfare,' she thought. She glanced at Ian's unresponsive face, but he did not return her glance.

"I'm off to bed," he said shortly. "If you'll excuse me, Susan, I'll—see you in the morning before I go."

Her heart sank.

"Oh, Ian, don't go, please," she said. "It's early yet. We could—"

"I'll see you in the morning," he repeated, and turned sharply away. "Goodnight. 'Night, Alan."

Susan looked after his rapidly-receding figure, then turned back to face Alan. She saw that he was smiling, and suddenly she ached to slap him—hard.

"Look, Alan," she said, her temper rising to boiling-point, "I'm tired of being a kind of shuttlecock between you two. Unless you'd like to tell me what it's all about, I'd rather dispense with your friendship. You see, I'm living with your father and mother, and—the others, and I'm happy with them, and I want it to go on like that." She stopped to get her breath, then continued, "I haven't any idea what this quarrel is about, and as I've said before it's none of my business. But you seem determined to drag me into it. What I mean is I can't help knowing that you and Ian just can't bear the sight of each other, and—"

"Oh, I wouldn't say that," Alan interrupted quietly.

"Well, anyway—" Susan started off again, but he cut in with,

"What you're trying to say, Sue, is that my presence is unwelcome, and that you'd rather have Ian's company than mine. Correct?"

"Oh!" She raised her hands, then let them fall in a gesture of exasperation. "I don't mean that at all, but—"

Alan moved forward a step. "I'm sorry," he muttered. "I know it's all my fault, and—look, let's go somewhere a little less public—" He glanced round at the crowding tents and big dining hall and the busy figures interweaving all about them. "Some place where we can talk. I've got the car here. Shall we go and sit in it, or perhaps you'd like a run out for a short while?"

"No, thanks," Susan said shortly. "I've had run enough for one day, also I have to be here to keep an eye on the children's tents."

"Well, I *would* like a talk with you, Sue. I—" he hesitated, then plunged on, "I'd like to—clear the air between us. You'll have to know the story some time, I guess, and I'd rather you heard it from me."

Susan looked at him for a moment, slightly bewildered, but at the same time relieved.

"Well, all right, Alan," she said. "Perhaps it would be a good idea. This—feud or whatever it is does seem to keep cropping up, whenever you meet up with any of your family, and it does seem a pity that you can't bring it out into the open. Perhaps if you told me all about it, I might think of a way to—to end it all."

Alan stared at her and then laughed aloud.

"Well, it would be just fine and bonzer if you could," he said half mockingly. "Anyway, let's go and sit in the car where we can be quiet."

Susan followed him, still feeling angry with him and also with Ian. 'He needn't have gone off like that,' she thought, and then came the further thought, 'I wonder if I'm going to hear the whole story at last? I hope so.'

In the darkness and privacy of the car Alan was silent for a while, and Susan did not help him. She was still half resentful at him coming here to-night of all nights, when she had hoped to resolve her misunderstanding with Ian. And now what would he think of the prompt appearance on the scene of his brother? He might even think it had all been arranged. And yet did it matter all that much? Susan sighed, and as if he had heard the slight sound Alan turned and reached for her hand.

"Sorry about all this, Sue," he said, "and it's a shame that Ian and I, and the boss, can't keep it to ourselves. But I guess it's gone too deep now and you just can't hide your feelings. I'm surprised that no one has mentioned it to you before this. Hasn't Melissa said—anything to you? Not that she knows the whole story."

"No." Susan shook her head. "And as for anyone else—well, Alan, the only people I meet are your family, Milton, the children, and of course the parents at the Wives' Club, and that's about all. So you see—"

"Yes." He paused, then laughed uneasily. "Er— it's not easy to tell, and you may think that I made too much of it, but—well, it all started with—a girl, a girl of mixed blood—in other words a half-caste aborigine. Her name was Charlotte, and—she was a lovely girl." He paused again and drew a hand across his eyes.

"And you were in love with her?" Susan said quietly.

"Well, I don't know; I'm not sure. You see, it all started innocently enough. She was the sister of one of our stockmen; they were orphans, and had been educated at the Mission School up near Darwin. She was an intelligent kid and—well, she wasn't having much of a time. I started helping her in various ways, you know, lending her books, and talking to her. She wanted to train for something or other, and I tried to advise her, but—well, my father found out about Charlotte and me—and there was one hell of a row. You must know by now what he's like; proud as Lucifer, particularly of his Highland Scottish ancestry. The very idea of me, his son, and one of the McQuarries, 'hobnobbing with an abo' (his own phrase, that) sent him almost round the bend. Up to then, Sue, I'd honestly never thought of Charlotte as anything more than a—friend; well, perhaps a little more than that, for she was very beautiful, and— alluring, but certainly nothing serious. But after that, it seemed as if he drove me to assert myself in the only way I knew how; I was only twenty at the time. And though I never actually said I intended marrying her, I deliberately let my father think so. Well—" Alan gave an involuntary laugh, "the old man nearly threw a fit. I thought he'd die of rage on the spot. Well, after he'd calmed down a bit he tried to bully me into promising that I'd have nothing more to do with Charlotte, and talked a lot of out-of-date bilge all about tradition and family pride, and the old country, etc, etc, but it cut no ice with me. I told him that it was my life and I'd live it in my own way. Lord, when I think of it now!" He stopped suddenly and Susan saw that his hands were clenched.

"What happened then?" she asked, feeling a certain amount of sympathy for Mr McQuarrie, but at the same time seeing Alan's point of view too.

"What happened then?" Alan's tone was bitter. "I'll tell you. I went back to medical school in Sydney. I wrote once to Charlotte, but had no reply. Well, the next time I went home I found that she and her brother had gone. I had another almighty row with Dad and accused him of having got rid of them. He denied it, as I knew he would, of course. I questioned the other stockmen, but they just all shook their heads. I made a few enquiries here, but with no result, and —well, that's all, the whole story."

A silence followed, then Susan asked,

"Well, what did you do then?"

"What else could I do?" he almost shot at her. "My time was limited. I had to return to Sydney still not knowing what had happened to Charlotte—and her brother."

"I'm sorry, Alan," Susan murmured, "I really am. You certainly had a raw deal. Were you—very much in love with her?"

There was a pause, and she saw him run a hand through his hair before replying.

"I—don't know," he said at last. "I liked Charlotte, and admired her very much. She was a fine person in every way, but—well, Sue, I honestly don't know. I sometimes think that if my dad hadn't tried to bulldoze me like I told you, the whole thing would have died a natural death. You see, though Charlotte was beautiful and intelligent she was still—half abo, and I had sense enough to know she wouldn't have fitted in with our way of life, and—" he paused again, "well, you see what I mean. The old man is really responsible for this state of affairs, and it's now four years, and the bitterness only seems to get worse."

"Do any of you try to make things better?" Susan asked. "Have you tried to understand and have it out with your father, for instance? You've admitted that you partly agree with him; and anyway, where does Ian come into it? though I guess he sided with your dad."

"Not only that," Alan said roughly, "it was he who told my father about me—and Charlotte. You see, he saw me with her, and—I was making love to her, I guess—oh, just in a mild way, but—"

"I see," Susan said quietly. "And what did he do?"

"Nothing; he just disappeared, and hardly spoke to me for days afterwards. Then things between Dad and me got even worse. Ma kept out of it; she knows the old man from experience." Alan paused for a second. "You ask if I've ever tried to have it out with him. No, I have not. I consider it's his place to make the first move."

Susan was silent for a moment.

"But, Alan," she said at last rather impatiently, "you have no proof that your father got rid of her. Perhaps she and her brother decided together that life would hold more for them somewhere else. If she was as intelligent as you say, and wanted to make something of her life, perhaps that's what she did. Have you made enquiries along those lines?"

He looked at her in some surprise. "No, I haven't, because it may be better not to," he said. "People change over the years. I think I have. I feel now that I must go forward and forget the past."

"Then for heaven's sake do the job thoroughly!" Susan cut in. "Make an effort to clear things up with your father. There are faults on both sides, you must know that; and as for Ian, he probably thought he was doing the best thing for you in the long run. As an elder brother he wouldn't want to see you making a mess of things at the beginning of your career and perhaps spoiling your whole life. I don't say it would, but—well, twenty's pretty young to tie oneself down. That's probably what Ian thought, don't you agree?"

Alan turned and looked at her, then broke into a laugh.

"And how old are you, Miss Wiseacre?" he asked.

"I don't come into it," she said quickly. "But—"

"Don't you?" he interrupted, and looked at her again. "Well, all right, then; I admit it's become a stupid quarrel, but what was said and done four years ago, by my father and brother, can't be undone—"

"Oh yes, it can," Susan interrupted. "You're not without blame, you know that. You deliberately let your father and Ian think something which was not really true—at the time, at least not altogether; and I can see, even if you can't, how they would see it, particularly your father, for letting the clan down, sort of thing. Oh, Alan—" she laid a hand on his arm, "can't you be a little generous and make the first gesture? Surely you can't want to cut yourself off from your family for the rest of your life?"

He moved impatiently. "No, of course I don't," he muttered. "But what do you suggest I should do—and don't expect me to do any boot-licking. After all, why should I?"

Susan sighed with exasperation. "Couldn't you come home for a weekend?" she said. "I mean let your parents know that you're coming, in a normal kind of way; not just descend out of the blue so that no one is prepared and everyone feels uneasy and uncertain. Couldn't you perhaps exchange a few words with your father on some sort of ordinary topic—and—"

Alan looked at her and laughed again.

"The situation does sound a bit grim when you put it like that," he said, then added after a short pause, "Would *you*—like me to come for a weekend?"

"Yes, of course I would," Susan said, and meant it. 'If I can help to straighten out this mess anything is worth it,' she was thinking. 'Even your friendship with Ian?' something seemed to ask, but she turned impatiently away from the answer, for where was that friendship now? It had apparently dissolved into nothing. She turned again towards Alan. "Well, will you do it?" she asked.

He hesitated for a moment, then said, "Well, all right. I guess it *is* the most sensible thing to do, I know that. Now—" his voice changed, and there was an excited note in it, "I've got some *real* news for you, Sue. Listen—" he squeezed her arm, "I've been accepted for the R.F.D.S. and I start at the beginning of the month on probation, of course."

"Oh, Alan!" her voice matched his own for excitement. "That's really super news, I *am* glad. Will you be based here at Alice Springs?"

In the half darkness she saw his head shake.

"No," his voice was regretful. "I wish I were. I shall be at the Cloncurry Area, much further north.

But it will be interesting work; takes in Darwin and Arnhem Land.”

“Alan!” Susan gripped his arm in sudden urgency. “Now this is a marvellous opportunity to start to straighten things out with your family. Couldn’t you get a weekend before you go; come up to Kanoch Doon and give your news to your father and mother? Would you, Alan? I’m sure your father would be so proud of you.” Alan looked at her and there was a long uneasy silence. “Please,” Susan urged softly.

“Why are you so—so interested in this business?” he asked at last.

“Why? Because—” She laughed. “I suppose I like you all so much, and—well, I just am, I guess. Anyway, will you?”

“Hmm—” he said slowly, then, “All right, Sue, I’ll do it. I’ll ask for a couple of days at the month end and come home. I’ll write, and you and Ma can prepare the fatted calf. Yes, I’ll tell them all the news, but don’t expect me to—”

“I won’t,” she interrupted. “Just write to say that you’re coming, and then—well, my guess is that everything will work out naturally.”

“I don’t know, Sue. It’s the sort of thing that—dies hard, you know.”

“Don’t think of it like that, Alan.” She paused, then added, “Thank you for telling me all this—and now I think I ought to go.”

“I *wanted* to tell you,” he said quietly. “I wanted to get the ground clear between us—if you know what I mean.”

Susan’s heart began to beat faster. Did she know

what Alan meant? And if so, what? And just where did Ian come in? "I'll drop you a line," he went on as she said nothing, "just to let you know how things are. Right? And now, if you really must—" and suddenly his arms were round her and she felt the warmth of his lips on hers. "Goodnight, darling Sue, and thanks for everything."

CHAPTER 7

SUSAN was feeling thoroughly bewildered as she made ready for bed in her small tent. She recalled Alan's words to her in the car, and wondered about their implication; and then she thought of Ian and wondered again uneasily if she were not getting into deep water between these two brothers. However, and here Susan drew a deep sigh of satisfaction, she *had* got Alan to promise that he would make the first move in healing the breach between himself and the rest of his family, and that was the important thing, she felt.

As she settled down on her camp bed her thoughts turned again, rather reluctantly, to Ian. What Alan had said about his brother's part in this family quarrel had come as an unpleasant shock to her. Why, Susan wondered, when Ian had seen Alan and the girl together, had he not tackled Alan about it before confronting his father with knowledge which he must have known would infuriate the older man? This was a facet of Ian's character which surprised her and indeed made her feel slightly contemptuous towards him. *Why* had Ian not first spoken to Alan about his conduct? The only explanation she could think of was that Ian was as proud and clan-conscious as his father; that the very idea of his brother making love to a half-caste girl would be enough to make him do everything he could to stop it once and for all. Of course—her eyelids were beginning to droop—Ian had not known all the facts about Charlotte, but even so —her lids closed for the last time, and she was asleep.

Ian left quite early the next morning. His manner to Susan was polite but cool. He did not ask any questions about his brother and Susan did not volunteer any information. She felt that there was none to give—yet. However, just before starting the car he surprised her by saying in an impersonal sort of voice,

"When you see Alan again, and of course you *will* be seeing him, remind him that he still has a home at Kanoch Doon." Susan stared at him, but before she could think of anything to say, he had put the car in gear and was off. Now what did Ian mean by that? she wondered. Did he also want to end this disastrous feud? She began to think a little better of him now. Yes, there must have been good reasons for what he had done.

However, for the next three days Susan's time was so full to the brim with excitement and interest that she had no time at all to ponder the affairs of Alan or his brother Ian. On that first morning all the children in the entire camp, with their teachers, gathered together at the big sports ground. They were given instructions and then everyone raced off towards a whole fleet of coaches. Susan knew there was to be an outing on the first day, but did not know where. Now Mary Ferguson told her that as they had visited Ayer's Rock last year, this time they were to have a picnic at Simpson's Gap.

"It's quite something," she told Susan. "Imagine a great—" then she broke off and laughed. "Never mind—just wait till we get there. By the way, can you come and have an evening meal with us? Alan says he can bring you out. You're free from seven, you know. We've got sitters-in; it's all organised."

"Oh, thanks," Susan smiled. "You should know, and if it's O.K. to leave camp I'd love to."

"Right. I'll brief Alan, then. Here we are, this is your coach."

The picnic to Simpson's Gap was an unqualified success with everyone. At first Susan noticed that the children were shy of one another and that each little 'school' was inclined to hang together, but very soon the self-consciousness wore off and the children began to really let themselves go, and it was quite heart-warming to see the spontaneous enjoyment of them all. They did not need entertaining, she thought, for it was enjoyment and novelty enough for them to be meeting and making friends with so many others like themselves.

"I can see now how important these big parties are," she said to one of the other teacher-supervisors. "It's like it is with grown-ups, too. We all learn from each other; and the more people one meets and talks to, the more one learns about living. Michael!" she broke off to call, then as the boy came running up, "Don't get too rough, and be careful climbing over those boulders. Where are the others from Kangaroo?"

Michael swept an arm across his heated face. "Oh, they're somewhere, Miss Susan," he said. "We don't stay together, we see enough of each other at home. I want to meet the other kids, and so does James and Mary and the rest."

"Well, that's all right," said Susan, "but don't overdo it. Remember we've got a whole day of sports and races to-morrow, with a barbecue in the evening."

"O.K., Miss Susan," and he raced off to join a group of boys.

Alan called for Susan in the evening at about seven-thirty and on the way out to the Ferguson bungalow she told him about the enjoyable day they had had at Simpson's Gap.

"It was just marvellous," she said. "Oh, how glad I am that I left Adelaide and that dull old job at Dalgetty's. I'm just loving it here and I'd like it to go on and on and on!"

Alan laughed and put a hand over hers. "You're a very stimulating person, Sue," he said. "Always bubbling over with enthusiasm, or sorting out other people's problems." He squeezed her hand lightly, then let it go.

"You should be bubbling over too," Susan told him. "With the prospect of that exciting job coming up."

"Well, yes, I am, of course. To tell you the truth—" he gave a shy sort of grin, "I can hardly wait. However, only two more weeks, and then—"

She looked at him. "Haven't forgotten your promise, have you?"

He shook his head. "No, I haven't; and I'll be writing to them soon. I'm—beginning to look forward to it. Seeing you at home, I mean."

Susan laughed a little self-consciously. "That's not the idea at all," she said, "but it'll be nice to see you, too. Ian's not very friendly lately." She looked at him and wondered what he would say to this, but he only said teasingly,

"I suppose that's the reason that I shall be welcome. What's got into brother Ian?"

Susan shrugged. "Well, I rather think *you* gave him the wrong idea," she said.

There was a pause, then Alan murmured,

"Oh, was it the wrong idea, I wonder?" Colour crept into her cheeks, but by now they had arrived at the Fergusons', so she was spared the necessity of a reply to Alan's half-question.

The evening passed swiftly in pleasant talk and a well-planned meal followed by coffee and liqueurs, but by eleven o'clock. Susan had difficulty in keeping her eyes open, and she saw that Mary was the same. She was relieved when goodnights were said and she and Alan were on their way back to the camp. He was very quiet and Susan herself was half asleep. But just before they reached the entrance to the camp and started to slow down, Alan looked at her and said,

"Sue, I want you to make me a promise."

Susan roused herself to look at him.

"Oh," she said sleepily, "what is it?"

He hesitated for a moment, then said rather sheepishly, "It's about this weekend of mine at Kangaroo. Er—don't mention it to Ian, what we discussed, I mean." He gave her a twisted sort of grin. "You see, I'd rather—"

"Oh, of course," Susan cut in quickly. "I wouldn't dream of saying anything to anyone. It's all up to you."

"Thanks, Sue." He stopped the car and got out. Susan followed. "I suppose this is where I say goodnight. You look half asleep already. Er—thanks for everything." He bent quickly forward and kissed her on the cheek, then climbed back into the car. "I'll be seeing you soon—I hope. 'Bye!"

The next two days were passed in a whirl of competitive sports, outings and barbecues and then the

Schools of the Air get-together came to an end with a grand combined camp-fire concert.

Kanoch Doon seemed very quiet to Susan and her pupils when they assembled again on the following Tuesday morning and sat waiting for the schools session to start from the R.F.D.S. Base. However, life soon fell into its ordinary routine and by the end of the week the children had stopped talking about the big event of the year and were already looking forward to the next treat, which was the Christmas party.

"It's real bonzer," Michael told Susan. "D'you know, Miss Susan, the whole of the R.F.D.S. Network is thrown open to the schools. Sometimes, of course, there's an emergency; an accident, or someone gets taken bad and has to have an operation, and then we have to go off the air; but it doesn't often happen."

"What do you do at this party?" Susan enquired, her curiosity aroused. "You can't very well play party games, or can you? Tell me about it."

"Oh, but we do have games, sort of—" Hilary said eagerly. "But we always start with some Christmas carols, then we have a game."

"D'you mean a kind of guessing game?"

"Yes, sometimes, but usually we play Consequences. You know, you write a name on a paper, then you turn the paper over, then the announcer calls out another question, and you write and turn the paper over again, and—well, you know."

"I see," said Susan. "Yes, I suppose it could be done. And then you read them out for the other schools to hear?"

Hilary nodded. "But the very bestest thing is the play," she said. "It's the same play for all the schools, and the teachers choose who'll take the parts. Then the ones who are chosen learn their parts—and we say it over the air to each other. It's real good. Last year we done—did, I mean—the play about the little fir tree."

Michael suddenly exploded into laughter. "'Member that girl Maggie something, from Big Tree Gap? She was supposed to be a fairy or something—fair cow she was!"

"Oh, Michael, that's not very polite," Susan said reprovingly.

Hilary suddenly started to jig up and down.

"You'll be hearing all about it soon, Miss Susan," she said. "They send you all about it from the Alice. You know, what characters you have to choose from us, and what the play is to be. D'you know, one year we had a musical play called 'Puss in Boots' and I had to sing a song. I wonder what it'll be this year. Oh, I do hope it's another musical and I have to sing again."

"Coo," James said disparagingly, "you weren't any great shakes. I think that girl from—" But Susan saw that Hilary was very near to tears and she hastened to intervene.

"Hilary sings very nicely," she said. "Now, listen, children." She glanced round the small group. "You know it will depend on you who gets chosen for the parts. It will be the ones who behave well in class, and try hard with their lessons."

"That don't follow," Michael put in. "You did oughter choose the kids who act best."

"Well," Susan said diplomatically, "you all act very well, so it won't be easy to choose, will it?" She glanced out of the window and saw Ian coming up from the men's quarters. He waved to someone on the front veranda of the house, but she could not see who it was. She sighed now and wished the day was over. Since her return to the homestead Ian's attitude to her had puzzled and angered her. He gave her no opportunity to do any explaining, and yet was quite pleasant and friendly when they met, which of course was every day almost. Doesn't he care at all? she asked herself. We were such good friends once.

Alan also puzzled her whenever she thought of their meeting in Alice Springs. She suspected that he had tried deliberately to give Ian the wrong impression, but when she recalled his words as they had sat in his car on that first evening of the school's get-together when he had told her all about the feud; and then had said, 'I *wanted* to tell you—I wanted to get the ground clear between us—if you know what I mean,' and then his kiss and embrace. Susan had wondered afterwards if Alan had really meant what his words had implied. And yet, she thought now, on the very next night when he had brought her home from the evening at the Fergusons' he had seemed strangely withdrawn.

Thinking it over again in her own room after school was over, she came to a surprising conclusion. Alan's behaviour did not worry her at all, in fact, she was not interested. Apart from the first little pleasurable thrill, her main interest was in helping to bring about a reconciliation between Alan and his father. But what of Ian? And as she asked herself this question the answer seemed to jump right at her. She was in love with Ian. Why hadn't she acknowledged it before, before they were both entangled in this web of misunderstanding? It was because she had been happy in their growing friendship, and had had no real thoughts of the future. It was not till that friendship had been withdrawn, with hardly a word spoken, that Susan knew what it had meant to her really. The loss of it had left her heart empty. She knew that her job here, interesting though it was, was not enough.

Well, what to do now? She wandered over to the door and stepped out on to the veranda; and as she did so she saw the two figures on the front veranda of the homestead almost opposite, and stepped quickly back. For the two people standing there very close together were Ian and Letty French. Susan watched them unashamedly, and at the same time was conscious of the most violent turmoil of feeling that she had ever experienced. Looking at Letty's laughing face upturned to Ian's, and her hand curved possessively round his arm, she had a strong urge to slap that smiling face and to push the hand away from his arm. As she watched, the two figures turned and walked slowly down towards the far end of the veranda and then disappeared from sight. If Susan had wanted proof of her own feelings towards Ian, this certainly provided it, for she had not known till this moment that she was capable of such a storm of emotion.

And now the question came again. What could she do? She walked back to her bed and sat on the edge. Was there anything she *could* do? Surely there must be something. Somehow, somewhere, she must get Ian to herself, and then force the issue. Perhaps, when Alan had paid his promised visit home and the quarrel had been settled, as surely it must be, then she might enlist Alan's aid. But almost immediately her mind rejected the suggestion. No, this was a matter between herself and Ian, and no one else. Perhaps—but even as she continued to explore possible ways of solving her problem something quite unexpected happened.

The very next morning Susan had a letter, and it was from Alan. 'Good, good,' she thought as she ripped open the envelope, 'this will surely be to announce his visit.' But it was not quite like that.

'Dear Susan (Alan wrote)

I must see you—at once. A most extraordinary thing has happened, and it puts quite a new complexion on what I spoke to you about recently. I intended to come home this weekend, but now—well, I just don't know. I feel I *must* talk to you again. It's very important, and I simply can't put it in a letter; there's too much of it to tell, and anyway I haven't much time. This is what I suggest. Next Saturday afternoon I could take the plane and meet you at Eighty-Mile. Could you get Melissa or Milton to run you in—make it a shopping expedition, perhaps? I could meet you at Romano's, and tell you everything, and then ask you a very important question. Please be there, Sue dear, I'm relying on you.

Love, Alan.'

Susan put the letter down on her knee, and saw that her hands were trembling. 'What an extraordinary letter!' she thought. 'What can have happened to Alan since I saw him?' She read the letter through a second time, then wondered uneasily what the important question could be. She fingered the pages of this strange missive, and then decided with some misgivings that she had better do as he asked. The more she thought about it the more curious she became. What could have happened, she wondered, to cause Alan to feel unsure as to whether he should come home or not? He must surely have discovered something which shed a new light on this quarrel. What could it be? She had a sense of bitter disappointment as she thought that whatever Alan had discovered it could not be something good, or he would not have felt that he could not come home. 'Well,' she thought, 'to-morrow's Saturday, and I'll see what Melissa says.' Luck was with Susan, for at breakfast Melissa announced that she was meeting a friend in Eighty-Mile and was starting off after lunch.

"I wonder if you could give me a lift into town," Susan asked. "I've got some shopping to do, and—"

"Of course," said Melissa, "I'll be glad of the company."

When Susan entered the hotel later that afternoon, the first person she saw was Alan. He was sitting at a table and watching the door. As soon as he saw Susan he rose with almost a bound and rushed to meet her. She saw that his face was pale and strained, but there was a light in his eyes that she had never seen there before. It was as if a veil had been removed, revealing a strange new Alan. Susan stared at him.

"Come over here," he said in a low tense voice. "It's quiet and we can talk. I've ordered tea. Thanks for coming, Sue. Was it O.K.?"

"Yes, Melissa was coming in anyway, so she gave me a lift. I'm meeting her again in a couple of hours. Now—" she looked across the table at him and saw again that strange new light in his eyes, "what's this extraordinary news, Alan?"

He took a deep breath, then blurted out,

"*The* most marvellous thing has happened, Sue. I can still hardly believe it. I've found—Charlotte!" Susan stared at him and he stared back at her, then he nodded. "Yes, it's true. She's a nurse, a trained nurse, at one of the little out-station hospitals that I visit sometimes, from the Darwin area. I went up with another chap just to have a look round, and I saw her in the ward. At first I hardly recognised her. She's— well, she's absolutely terrific, Sue! She's—" He spread his hands and stared into Susan's amazed face.

"Oh, Alan!" She was breathless with excitement. "What a wonderful thing to happen; when you thought you'd lost all touch with her, and what a moment when you recognised her! What did she say?"

"Well," he laughed excitedly, "look, let's have our tea, shall we? Here it is. Will you pour?" When the waiter had gone he continued, "I certainly didn't waste any time, I can assure you. I managed to meet her when she came off duty. And then, of course, I asked her why she and her brother Tom had left our place so suddenly and without a word to anyone. Well, she hesitated for a long time. I could see that she was unwilling to say anything that might cause a row; but I kept on, Sue, I felt I had to get to the truth of it. Then she told me." He stopped abruptly, and Susan waited, almost holding her breath.

"It wasn't a bit what I'd thought," Alan said at last, and then he smiled at her, a smile of complete happiness, it seemed to her. "I was wrong, Sue, wrong all along the line. Wrong about Dad, wrong about Ian, wrong about everything. Dad had nothing to do with Charlotte and Tom leaving. It was their decision, at least it was Tom's. You see, Sue, all the time when I was thinking of Dad and his pride, it never for one moment occurred to me that others might feel the same; Tom, for instance. Sue, the chap who saw Charlotte and me on that particular night was not my brother Ian, but Charlotte's brother Tom. They're much of a height, and it was dusk—" He paused again and Susan saw the shame on his face. "Well, Tom decided that his sister, of whom he was very fond, was not going to be the—plaything of the boss's son; so, quite quietly, and without saying anything to anyone, he left, taking Charlotte with him. Well, Sue, you can imagine how—petty—I felt when she told me that. Tom is now head stockman at a big place near Darwin, and Charlotte—" he paused once more and Susan saw the glow in his eyes—"Charlotte had been helped by the Mission to take her nurse's training, and she is now fully qualified. I feel very proud of her—and pretty small myself. Sue—" he leaned across the table, "I want you to meet her just as soon as we can fix it. You'll love her."

Susan smiled into his eager face. "I'm sure I shall," she said, and then there was a sudden, rather uneasy silence betwen them. "Alan, what about your father, and Ian?" Susan asked at last. "Are you coming home before you start your job, as you said you would?"

"Well now, that's just it," he said, looking away from her. "Of course I want to, now more than ever, but—"

"Oh, but you must!" she broke in. "Don't you see, Alan? Why, you've wronged your father and brother. They must have been bitterly hurt, especially Ian who had absolutely nothing to do with it." She stared into his eyes and waited.

"Yes, I know all that," Alan admitted. "And of course I want to clear matters up, almost more than anything else; apologise and the rest of it, especially to Ian, but—well, I said 'almost more than anything else' just now, and that's what I meant. You see, Sue, there's a big snag, a helluva big snag."

"You mean—Charlotte?"

"Yes, Charlotte. Sue—" he put a hand over hers, and squeezed it hard, "I'm going to marry her. I haven't asked her yet, but—" he shook his head and a half smile played round his lips, "I think I know what her answer will be. She's my girl, and always was, and we know it now, both of us. But there's Dad. He'll never think of Charlotte as anything but an abo. You probably know by now just how narrow and out-of-date he is in matters of this kind, and how proud he is of his Highland Scottish ancestry. Of course I shall write and tell Ian, *and* of course apologise. I might even ask him to meet me here, but the boss is a different kettle of fish altogether. I can't see us ever getting out of this muddle. You know, Sue—" he looked at her thoughtfully, "I think the reason I've been so bitter about him was Charlotte. Though I told you that we were just friends, and that I'd come to think that perhaps it was all for the best—" he paused for a moment, then continued speaking in a slow halting way, "losing her, I mean—deep down I knew that she was the only girl for me, and I blamed Dad and almost hated him for it. Now, of course, I feel a perfect swine. What do you think, Sue?"

"I think you should tell him, Alan, about Charlotte—and apologise, of course."

"Tell him?" Alan's tone was incredulous. "Just

like that? You evidently still don't know my father. He just couldn't take——"

"Listen," Susan interrupted, "perhaps *you* don't know your father—completely. He's had time, in four years, to get used to an idea; he must have thought about it in all its aspects. He can't possibly *want* this feud to go on, I feel sure of that. Sometimes he looks very sad. You're his son, Alan, and he doesn't want to lose you altogether. That's what it must seem like now. And there's your mother to think of. Please, Alan, tell them." She leaned across the table and stared into his face. "Look, tell them first about your new job; that should soften *him* up, and then—about Charlotte." She paused, then added quickly, "Alan, I've got an idea. Why not write to say you're coming home to give them some important news and that you're bringing a friend—Charlotte?"

He gave a short laugh. "If she'd come," he said rather grimly. "Charlotte's like her brother Tom; plenty of pride. No, Sue, I just couldn't risk it. Why, I haven't even told her how I feel about her, so——"

"Well, tell her, then," Susan interrupted. "Go and see her and tell her, and ask her to come home with you to meet your parents. It's a risk for both of you, I know, but if she loves you she'll do it. Don't you see, Alan? You say she's proud—well, she'll *want* to be accepted by your family. Didn't you say she had changed out of all recognition? Did your father ever actually meet her when she lived near here?"

He shook his head. "She wasn't exactly on his visiting list," he said with a wry smile.

"Well, there you are!" Susan voice was triumphant. "He probably won't even recognise her. Have you a photograph?"

Alan smiled sheepishly and dived into his pocket. "She gave me this," he said, and passed the small square over to Susan. She picked it up and studied it with keen interest. So this was Charlotte. It showed a slim girl in trim nurse's uniform. It was in colour and Charlotte's skin looked very little darker than Susan's own. Large dark eyes looked out from a heart-shaped face, and the only sign that Susan could detect of aborigine blood was in the generously full-lipped mouth.

"Oh, Alan," she said, "how could anyone object to a girl like this? Why, she's quite beautiful!"

He looked gratified as he took the picture back and glanced at it with adoring eyes.

"Well now," he said presently, and looked reflectively at Susan, "you're surely not suggesting that I should introduce her to my family without telling them who—"

"Of course not." Her voice was indignant. "But there's no need to tell them right off, is there? Let them meet her, and let them see for themselves how suitable she is, and how she fits in; and then, after you've told them about your wonderful new job, take the plunge. It's worth it, I think, and surely Charlotte will too. After all, you have nothing to lose, have you? You couldn't be more estranged than you are. You might even enlist Ian's aid, if you could manage to tell him first. It's an idea, isn't it?"

Alan sat looking moodily at the table, then he took a long drink from his cup and set it down empty. He looked at Susan and grinned.

"You've certainly set me something," he said. "And I did ask your advice, *and* of course you're right. I'll have to think it over, and of course see Charlotte as soon as possible, and see what she says after—" He grinned again. "Look, pal, I'll write to you after I've thought it well over, and tell you what I've decided on. O.K.?"

"O.K. it is," Susan agreed, then looked at her watch in sudden alarm. "Hey, I'll have to fly if I'm not to miss Melissa." She stood up. "You will write, Alan, and soon?"

CHAPTER 8

AS Susan bade Alan a hurried goodbye and walked out of the hotel into the street, the uppermost thought in her mind was, 'So that was Alan's important question; whether to tell his father about Charlotte', and then she wanted to laugh at herself and what she had imagined the question would be. 'I must be getting terribly conceited,' she thought ruefully, but was conscious at the same time of a tremendous feeling of relief, of freedom. Though she still had no idea of how to break down the barrier between herself and Ian, yet the fact that the situation between herself and Alan was now made clear and would soon be out in the open seemed to make everything much more hopeful. She waved to Melissa whom she saw leaning against the car at the top of the street.

"Done all your shopping?" the latter enquired as Susan came hurrying up. They both climbed into the car and Melissa started up the engine. Susan nodded and hoped that Melissa would not notice the almost total absence of parcels. But the other girl was too full of her own concerns. She bubbled over with excitement as she told Susan of the visit she had paid to Mike Lingard, a vet whom she had met at the house of a friend.

"He's going to show me over his animal hospital," she said. "And he's told me I can come along and help whenever I like. I think I'm going to be a vet."

"Changed your mind about being a teacher, then?" Susan smiled. "Have you told your mother?"

Melissa tossed her head. "Oh, I guess Ma knows," she said. "Anyway, it was Dad's idea to start with."

Susan was silent, and Melissa added, "But it's not mine, not now, and I'm going to tell him so. I'm going to live my life as I want it."

"Well, I should think you could be very useful on the farm, as a vet, I mean."

"Stay on the farm?" Melissa's voice was scornful. "Not me! I shall set up practice in Sydney or Melbourne and make pots of money."

"There are far more animals out here among the farms," Susan observed. "All you'd get in Sydney or Melbourne would be pampered poodles and lap-dogs."

"Hmm—" Melissa mused after a short pause, "I never thought of it like that. Anyway, it's a vet's life for me. D'you know, Sue—" and off she went again about Mike Lingard and what he had said to her.

"Sure it's the animals and not the vet?" Susan asked her teasingly.

The car turned in at last at the wide gates leading to Kanoch Doon.

"Oh, by the way," Melissa said in a studiously casual kind of voice, "I met Letty French and she's coming over to-morrow; she told me to tell Ian." She glanced sideways at Susan, then added, "She seems to be doing rather well lately in that direction."

"In what way?" Susan asked, though she could feel the hot colour rising to her cheeks under Melissa's glance.

"Oh, she's nuts on Ian, as you probably know." Melissa brought the car to a standstill with a flourish of gravel under the wheels. "But brother Ian's not easy. He's past what I call the soft age. You know, when they think girls are wonderful mysteries. Ian's pushing up thirty, y'know—almost middle-aged. He can't be rushed into things now."

"Good thing he can't," Susan remarked shortly.

Melissa looked at her. "At one time I thought he was quite taken with you," she observed, watching Susan's face. "What happened?"

"Why, nothing," Susan said impatiently. "You must have been mistaken. Anyway—" she stopped abruptly, for she had been about to add, 'it's no business of yours,' but thought better of it.

"Yes, I guess I must have been," Melissa said airily as she climbed out of the car. "But Ian's quite a catch, you know. Lots of girls have tried to put the handcuffs on him."

Susan could not help laughing, and suddenly she felt quite light-hearted, for if what Melissa said was true then Ian would not be likely to be rushed into something against his will. But then she thought of Letty French and felt less happy about it. Letty was a very determined girl; it showed in her face and in those compelling light blue eyes of hers.

Melissa threw her a shrewd glance.

"Dad *and* Ma would like Ian to get married," she said, and leapt lightly up the veranda steps. "To the right girl, of course. See you later, Sue."

"Thanks, and thanks for the lift, Melissa!" Susan called a trifle belatedly, and as she walked to her own room she wondered if Melissa were giving her a word of warning. However, when she went up to the house for the evening meal Mrs McQuarrie told her that Ian would be away for two or three days at the cattle sales. Susan was conscious of an instant sense of relief; the relief of knowing that for a few days at least she could stop wondering about how she could get Ian to herself and then persuade him to talk, for Susan was determined to break through this web of misunderstanding that seemed to envelop them both. Then, as she thought of her secret meeting with Alan and of his astounding news, she began to feel almost light-hearted again. Surely after Alan had been home and been reconciled with his family and Charlotte accepted Ian would know then that there was not, and never had been, anything between herself and his brother. So Susan's thoughts ran. 'Yes,' she told herself, 'everything will work out right as soon as Alan comes home.'

The next day happened to be the occasion of the Wives' Club of the Air. Susan always enjoyed these meetings. Some of her pupils' mothers attended, and it gave her an opportunity to talk to them and to see what they thought of the progress made by their children. Up to now they had all expressed complete satisfaction, and Susan had had a sense of quiet triumph. These meetings were always stimulating to her, and there was always an interesting speaker. This time, Mrs McQuarrie told Susan when she entered the kitchen to supervise the children's dinner, the speaker was to be a matron from one of the up-country hospitals, and was supposed to be very good.

Afternoon school over, Susan hurried over to the house. The usual bustle was going on; chairs being moved around, the chink of china as cups and saucers were arranged on trays, and from the kitchen the delicious aroma of baking scones and cakes.

Everything went off as before. First, the theme song; then the minutes were read. While this was going on Susan slipped out quietly to the kitchen to butter the scones and take the cake out of the oven. When she returned, the guest speaker was just about to begin her talk. She had a pleasant voice, Susan thought, leisurely and easy to listen to. She spoke first very briefly of the administration of the hospital, then of the patients, and lastly of her staff. Susan listened with great interest; then suddenly she shot up in her chair and stared in amazement at the transceiver. For, of the several names which the matron had mentioned, one had seemed to leap out at her. She wondered if she had heard aright, and listened with bated breath. Yes, it came again in the matron's clear low voice.

"Yes, I am indeed fortunate in my staff," she said, "and I would like particularly to mention Staff Nurse Charlotte Moore who has been with us for the past year. She is a really dedicated nurse, and though she is only twenty-three, I would have no hesitation at all in delegating any duty to her, she is so thoroughly reliable. I would like to add that Staff Nurse Moore is proud to be of mixed aborigine and Scottish blood, and all I can say in conclusion is that it's a pretty good mixture—and *I* should know!"

The rest of the meeting passed for Susan in a kind of daze. She was conscious of the trays being passed round, she heard the chatter going round about her, she even rose and collected trays and took them to the kitchen, but above all, she was conscious of the comments from the women on the Matron's talk. "The abos are as intelligent as anyone else," one woman said, "and thank goodness the country's waking up to the fact. Look what that Matron said about the nurse. She must be a fine girl."

"Yes, a girl to be proud of," Mrs McQuarrie suddenly put in, and Susan looked quickly at her. 'She knows—she knows who Charlotte Moore is,' Susan thought, and excitement began to surge through her. 'Somehow I must let Alan know, for this could help enormously. Somehow I must tell him about this speaker and what she said of Charlotte; also his mother's comment. Surely nothing could go wrong now? Why, this family should be proud to welcome such a daughter-in-law!' She drew a deep breath and looked about her, and saw that nearly everyone had gone.

Later that evening as Susan and Mrs McQuarrie were busy putting the room to rights and washing up the crockery, Susan was suddenly tempted to speak to the older woman about Charlotte, or perhaps in some way lead Mrs McQuarrie to introduce the subject, but then she put it away from her. No, it's Alan's affair, she thought, and he must see it through. It would be frightful if something I said spoilt it all. Oh no, I mustn't risk it. I must just hope and pray that Alan will soon be here and then everything will be sorted out. But what I *can* do is write and tell him about this matron at Charlotte's hospital.

But fate was to take a hand in Alan and Charlotte's affairs. When Susan went into breakfast the following morning she found Mrs McQuarrie looking tired and worried.

"You did too much yesterday at the meeting," Susan told her. "Now, you just sit down and let Melissa and me do the breakfasts."

But Mrs McQuarrie shook her head.

"No, it's nothing to do with me," she said. "It's Dad. He's not well at all. He couldn't sleep all night, and this morning he's complaining of pains in the chest. I've made him stay in bed, though it was a job to make him do it. He looks bad, Sue, his face is quite grey; so I've got Melissa to put in a call to the Royal Flying Doctor Base to ask the doc to come and see him. I haven't told Dad that. He'd be furious. He says all he needs is a bit of a rest, but—well, I'm worried about him."

"Oh, I am sorry, Auntie Mac," said Susan. "Is there anything I can do? Look, I could help with the breakfasts, couldn't I? You sit down and let me cope with it. I know all about cooking. You see, I looked after my father for nearly four years—till he married again."

Mrs McQuarrie smiled at the eager face. "Oh, thank you, dear," she said. "I must say I do feel a bit washed out. What with Dad moaning and groaning, and twisting and turning, I didn't get much sleep either. I'll be glad when the doc comes."

"When do you expect him?" Susan asked, going towards the kitchen door, then pausing for a reply.

"Well, it shouldn't be very long. Those little Flying Doctor planes cover hundreds of miles in no time at all."

"I'll get on with the breakfast, then," Susan said. "I've got heaps of time before school starts." Within a few minutes the appetising smell of frying bacon, eggs, toast and coffee spread through into the next room.

"Goody!" grinned Melissa, coming to the door. "That smells real bonzer, Sue. I got my call through, 'Ma," she called over her shoulder. "I guess the doc will be here soon."

Her mother sighed. "Well, I hope you're right," she said. "Where's Milton? Have you told him about your father?" Melissa nodded. "Ah, here he is. Now, let's get breakfast over, and then I'll take something in to Dad, and break the news to him that the doc's on his way. He won't like it, I know." Everyone sat down round the table and got on with the meal in a subdued silence, and presently Susan glanced at her watch.

"I'll have to go now," she said. "But, Auntie Mac, do let me know if there's anything I can do, won't you?"

Mrs McQuarrie smiled and patted her hand. "I will," she said, "and thanks a lot, Sue."

Morning school seemed very long that day to Susan. She was worried about Mrs McQuarrie and about the boss; also about the fact that Ian should be away just at this time. She wondered if it would be possible for them to get in touch with him. As she supervised the lessons and kept the children's attention directed to the voice of the teacher coming over the air her ears were on the alert all the time for the distant sound of the flying doctor's plane. But it was not till she was on the point of dismissing her small school for the lunch break that she heard the faint drone getting steadily louder. She glanced out of the window and saw it in the distance. The drone became a brief roar, and then came the regular phut-phut of the engine as it touched down at the runway. Susan gave the children the signal for dismissal, warning them to keep away from the plane, then made her way over to the front veranda just as Mrs McQuarrie appeared at the living room door.

"Sue," she called, "go down and meet the doc, will you, dear? Lord only knows where Melissa is, though I told her particularly to stay around the house. I don't feel I can leave Dad just at the moment; he's very restless."

"Of course," said Susan. "I'll go right now." She turned and ran back down the steps of the veranda and made her way to the runway at the back of the homestead. As she came in sight of the now grounded plane she saw that the pilot or the doctor was already climbing out; and as she drew nearer she thought for a fleeting moment that the figure looked familiar. Then she stopped for a moment and stared before running forward to meet him. For the man who had just descended from the Cessna was—Alan McQuarrie. 'Alan, of all people,' Susan thought. 'And yet why not? Alan is a flying doctor now, though still on probation; and the Base at Alice Springs would have known at once on receipt of Melissa's message that the patient was Alan's father. So what more natural than that he should be detailed for this medical call?'

"Alan!"

"Sue!"

They exclaimed at exactly the same moment, and then over Alan's shoulder Susan saw the second figure preparing to descend the ladder—and it was the figure of a woman.

"Look, Sue," Alan began in a rapid undertone, and half turning towards the ladder as he spoke, "I can't explain anything yet; no time.. But—" he hurried back to the ladder, drawing the dazed Susan with him—"this is—Charlotte Moore, my nurse."

Susan gasped, then looked at the girl standing

there, at the big dark eyes, the gentle full-lipped mouth and the warmly-glowing skin, and thought she had never seen anyone quite as lovely as Charlotte Moore.

Charlotte smiled at Susan, showing dazzling white teeth.

"Hello," Susan said breathlessly.

"Hello," responded Charlotte, and then they both laughed.

"Susan, how is Dad?" Alan asked. He listened to her reply, then slipped one hand through Charlotte's arm and the other through Susan's. "I'll tell you later on how I—we come to be here," he whispered in Susan's ear. "But just now I'm the flying doctor and Charlotte is my nurse, see? She didn't want to come at first, but I persuaded her."

The three were walking up to the house now and Susan saw Mrs McQuarrie waiting at the corner of the veranda. She glanced sideways at Alan and saw that his face had gone pale beneath the tan. "Leave me and Charlotte with Ma," he whispered to her. "I'll see you later, Sue."

He let go her arm, but as she turned away Susan glimpsed the look of incredulous joy on Mrs McQuarrie's face as Alan bent forward and put both arms around her.

Susan's breath was coming in excited gulps as she ran back to the schoolroom. She tidied up, checked up on the children's whereabouts, went to her own room to wash her hands, then started off to the house. As she went up the veranda steps she could hear Melissa in the kitchen and went in to join her.

"Well, what d'you know?" Melissa turned from

the big cooker to stare at Susan. "Alan's here, did you know?"

Susan nodded. "I met the plane," she said.

"Oh? Well, I bet you got as big a surprise as I did. I saw him for only a minute before he went in to Dad. There was a nurse with him. Alan must be on the staff at the Alice, but why ever didn't he let us know, I wonder?"

"Perhaps he's only just started there," Susan said. "Your call must have been quite a shock to him—his own father, I mean."

"Yes." Melissa looked thoughtful. "Dad's better," she said, then giggled. "He's wild as a bunch of brumbies at Ma, for getting a doctor, but gosh, I'd love to have seen his face when Alan walked in!" She giggled again. "He'll have to do as Alan tells him now, won't he? He'll *love* that! I say, Sue, that nurse of Alan's is a right looker, isn't she? I wonder if he picked her. I wouldn't be surprised if there's a drop of abo blood there, but she's certainly a beaut."

"She certainly is," Susan agreed, then added over-casually, "Where is she now?"

"Where do you think? In with Alan and Dad, of course. She is the nurse, you know."

Susan's heart had missed a beat at Melissa's words. Would Douglas McQuarrie recognise Charlotte? But perhaps he had never actually seen her before. It was unlikely that he would ever have occasion to meet his stockmen's female relatives. She tried to picture Charlotte as the sister of an aborigine stockman, and it seemed to her almost incredible as she recalled the beautiful, proud yet gentle face and the trim figure in its spotless white uniform.

The children came trooping in at this moment and Melissa decided to give them their lunch at once. Susan had hers with them and then took them all with her back to the schoolroom.

"I want you to be very quiet till afternoon school," she told them. "The boss isn't well, and the doctor is with him now. We can all help by being quiet. I want you to choose a book to read, or a piece of handwork, or just have a rest. Right?"

The children entered into the spirit and settled down quite happily. Susan had seen nothing of Alan or Charlotte or Mrs McQuarrie since breakfast time and she was finding it very difficult to contain her curiosity as to what was happening up at the house. How was the boss faring? she wondered. Melissa had said he was better and Susan hoped she was right. How had he reacted to the appearance of his own son as the flying doctor? And what of Charlotte? Was she just the nurse to him, or *had* he recognised her? It was possible, of course.

Afternoon school came to an end at last, and Susan went thankfully to her own room to shower and change. She had just finished dressing and was powdering her face when there was a knock at the door. Susan opened it quickly and saw Alan. He grinned at her.

"Can I come in?" he asked, then as she waved him to a chair he looked at her and laughed. "What a day!" He threw himself into the chair and stretched out his legs. "But we're staying the night. Normally we'd have left by now, but I've been on to Base. They know it's my home, so they've stretched a point." He heaved a sigh and leant his head against the back of the chair.

"Oh, good!" said Susan. "How *is* the boss?" She sat down near him, and he nodded reassuringly.

"Much better," Alan told her. "But he'll have to take things easy from now on. It's his heart, I'm afraid. But there's no immediate cause for worry."

"I'm so glad," Susan said, then added impulsively, "Oh, Alan, I'm dying to hear about—oh, just everything I guess. How you—managed it all, and Charlotte, and—go on, *please* tell me before I bust." Alan laughed aloud. He was looking relaxed and almost happy, Susan thought, then waited impatiently for him to speak. He smiled at her.

"Well, to begin at the beginning—" he said. "That's always a good place to start, isn't it?"

"Go *on*," she begged, "or I'll hit you!"

He laughed again. "Oh, all right, here goes," he said. "When I left you at Eighty Mile after our talk, I—went to see Charlotte straightaway and told her everything. We also—got engaged."

"Oh, congratulations," Susan smiled. "Yes, go on."

"Well," Alan said, "it wasn't easy to persuade her to come here with me, and in fact we were still arguing about it when Melissa's message came through. I'm on probation at the Alice, but of course I asked if I could go as it was my father. Charlotte was off duty from her hospital, but I managed, after a struggle, to get her to come along. It's been pretty awful, Sue—first not knowing what was wrong with the old man, and then realising that there would have to be a complete showdown; if he were well enough to take it."

"Have you said anything to him yet?" Her tone was breathless with interest.

Alan nodded and laughed, then paused to extract

a cigarette from the packet and offer one to Susan. He lit both then continued.

"Well, of course, the first thing he wanted to know was what I was doing here at home, and then I told him about my job. It was a bit grim. You see, Sue, over the years, we'd got so much into the way of—well, not trusting each other, I suppose, that it was very difficult at first. *And* of course I had to be careful not to excite him—the heart, you see. Well, anyway, I could see that he was really pleased about it all, in his queer reserved way. Y'know, he's one of these inarticulate people; finds it almost impossible to express his feelings in words. Ian's the same."

'Is he?' Susan thought. 'I must remember that.'

"Well, anyway," Alan continued, "we began to get on better after that. He asked me all sorts of questions about the job, and where I was living, and we both began to be more at ease with each other. Then—" he drew on his cigarette and Susan could see that he was living this difficult patch all over again. "I—er— I told him that I was sorry about—the quarrel, and all the misunderstandings. I even said it was all my fault." He looked at Susan and grinned crookedly. "Go on, laugh! And then he said, no, it was his fault; that he should have trusted me not to make a fool of myself. Well, that was getting on to dangerous ground again, so I said nothing to that, and— well, so far, everything's fine. He even called me 'Al', which is something he hasn't done for a very long time. Dear old Ma is as pleased as a dog—I mean bitch—with two tails. So—" he looked across at Susan and laughed.

"But," she said urgently, "what about Charlotte? Where was she while all this was going on? Haven't you said anything to him yet—about her?"

"No, I haven't, for I felt it wasn't the right time. But he has seen her, for she helped me in the examination."

"He's seen her?" Susan stared at him. "He—didn't recognise her, then?"

"Oh no, I knew there was no danger of that," Alan said, a trifle impatiently. "Otherwise I'd never have taken the chance. If Dad's ever seen Charlotte before, when they were near here, I mean, he'd never recognise her now, I knew that. No, Sue, I've said nothing yet; it would be too risky just now. He's asleep now and seems almost his old self. When he wakes, we'll see. I'd certainly like to get the whole thing off my chest at last, and so would Charlotte, but I'll have to wait for the right moment."

"Yes, of course," Susan agreed. "Alan, I'm so glad the quarrel with your father is over at last. At least you must feel very happy about that. What about your mother? Have you said anything to her—about Charlotte? Where is she now, by the way?"

"She's been with Ma most of the time, and is with her now. They're getting on fine. I don't know whether Ma suspects, but that doesn't worry me. She was never so bigoted as the old man. When I left the two of them they were swapping recipes in the kitchen. Oh, and Mum told me about the talk at the galah session a few days ago." He smiled at Susan. "Somehow I don't think she would mind a bit."

Susan laughed and clasped her hands in satisfaction.

"I've got a hunch that everything's going to turn out fine," she said. "And when Ian comes back——"

"A second most abject apology," Alan said, grimacing, "though I won't mind making myself into a doormat for Ian. He's a good chap and was always a good big brother to me. He must often have wondered what had got into me."

"Oh, I don't know," Susan said thoughtfully. "He might have partly guessed, you know. After all, he sees much more of the stockmen, and knows them probably much better than your father. Ian might have heard, or even seen something. But the important thing is that it was not Ian who told your father." She stopped speaking suddenly, looked across at Alan, then asked, "Alan, who *did* tell your father? I know that it was Tom and not Ian who saw you with Charlotte that night, but was it *Tom* then who told the boss?"

There was a brief silence, then Alan slowly nodded his head.

"Yes, it was Tom," he said. He looked away from her and she saw that a flush had risen to his cheeks. "And it makes me feel like—a worm. It happened after I went back to Sydney to college. Tom came to see my father. He told Dad what he'd seen, and then —I got all this from Charlotte—he told Dad that his sister was too good to become the 'woman' of his son, and that he was taking Charlotte away. He told Dad that he was a good boss but that his son, meaning me, was no good for his sister, or words to that effect. Sue, it must have been the first time that Dad, or I for that matter, had realised that every decent man, whatever his colour, has his pride. Well, Dad paid Tom off and that was the end of it. I guess he thought it was the best thing that could have happened. Later on, when I came home, he said nothing to me about Tom's visit; probably thought it was better to let sleeping dogs lie." Alan paused for a moment. "Perhaps he was right. You see, I still didn't know my own mind, then. I understood what the old man felt about abos, because in a way I felt the same, I'd been brought up like that, y'see. And yet I couldn't seem to forget Charlotte. I suppose I really loved her all the time, but wouldn't face up to it."

Susan smiled across at him.

"And now it's all working out," she said. "Oh, Alan, I can't tell you how happy I am about it all! I feel in my bones that it's going to be a case of 'And they all lived happy ever after'."

Alan laughed, then rose to his feet.

"Well, ready to eat?" he asked, then as Susan nodded, "Come on then, let's go and find it!"

CHAPTER 9

THEY found Charlotte still sitting in the kitchen with Mrs McQuarrie, who was now busy preparing the evening meal. Charlotte smiled shyly at Susan. Alan talked to them for a while, then turned to his mother.

"I'll just go in and have a look at Dad," he said. "Is he still sleeping?" His mother nodded, and Susan noticed that she was looking very much happier and more relaxed. Alan went to the door while Susan started to prepare the salad.

"I'm trying to persuade Charlotte to stay over the weekend," Mrs McQuarrie told Susan, and the latter saw the light of a new-found happiness in her eyes. "Dad's taken quite a fancy to her; and Alan could pick her up on his next visit. I wish he could stay a little longer too, but he says he has to leave in the morning."

"It is very kind of you, Mrs McQuarrie," Charlotte said in that dark-brown velvety voice of hers. "But I think I must ask Alan's advice before—"

"What about?" His voice came from the door as he shut it carefully behind him. "Dad's still sleeping," he added in an aside to his mother. "His colour is fine, and his pulse quite steady and strong. He'll be O.K. now, Ma, but he'll have to slow up a bit from now on; you know that, don't you? He's over sixty, isn't he? This mild attack is a warning, and it'll be up to you to see that he heeds it. Now—" he turned to Charlotte, "what's the advice you need, my love?" The colour rose to her cheeks at this open word of endearment and she glanced quickly at Mrs McQuarrie, who merely smiled.

"Your mother has kindly invited me to stay over the weekend," Charlotte said. "But——"

"Why, that's a marvellous idea," said Alan, smiling at his mother. "I shall feel quite happy now about leaving Dad, even though it's only for a couple of days. Charlotte knows more than I do," he added with a grin. "Yes, you couldn't have a better person in charge than Staff Nurse Charlotte Moore. Ma, I'm hungry!"

And the next morning, very early, the Flying Doctor plane called for Alan and he returned to the Base at Alice Springs. His father was sleeping peacefully when he left and only opened his eyes about half an hour later when Charlotte went quietly in to see that all was well. She came out smiling.

"He is looking very well," she told Mrs McQuarrie. "He wants to get up, but I told him not just yet; not till this evening, and then for only a short time."

Milton and Melissa came in at that moment and the usual breakfast bustle began. The meal was perhaps half-way through when everyone heard it—the sound of a heavy fall from the bedroom. Charlotte shot to her feet and reached the door almost in one movement. Mrs McQuarrie rushed after her into the room. The others waited indecisively at the table and then heard Charlotte call for Milton. He was across the room in one stride.

"Help me to lift him," Susan heard her say a second later, and her voice was as calm and unhurried as if nothing had happened. Susan went to the open door and waited in case there was anything she could do to help, and Melissa followed her with a scared look on her face. The two girls peered round the edge of the door and saw Douglas McQuarrie lying by the side of the bed. The bedside cabinet door was wide open and his slippers were beside him. It seemed obvious that he had been attempting to get out of bed.

"Take his shoulders," Charlotte instructed Milton, "and I will take his legs." Mrs McQuarrie hovered round with white anxious face. Between them they got the big inert body back on to the bed. Susan heard him groan, and was conscious of heartfelt relief. She glanced at Melissa and knew she had had the same dread thought in her mind. She looked again at the sick man. His face was glistening with sweat and he was gasping for breath. Charlotte turned for a swift moment, saw Susan and motioned her to come in.

"Help me to lift his shoulders," she said to her, and then motioned to Mrs McQuarrie to pack the pillows behind him. "We must keep his head high. Milton—" she turned to the young man, "get the oxygen trolley from the corner there," she nodded her head towards it and he quickly trundled it over. Susan watched in silent admiration as Charlotte rapidly placed the trolley in position, quietly tested the flow of oxygen, then placed the B.L.B. mask in position all in a matter of minutes. The rest of them stood round in readiness and watched as Charlotte took the sick man's wrist in her hand and felt his pulse. The breathless silence in the room was broken only by Douglas McQuarrie's painful gasps for breath. Susan watched his face with shocked yet fascinated eyes. But after a few seconds only it seemed to her that the gasps became less laboured, his face was less white under the deep tan, and the awful blue ring round his mouth was slowly fading. Charlotte was still holding his wrist.

"He is coming round now," she said softly. She glanced up at Mrs McQuarrie who was standing beside Susan with her hands clasped tightly across her breast. "Please bring brandy and water." Mrs McQuarrie turned and hurried out of the room. "Now," Charlotte turned to Susan, "please hold his arm—firmly," and Susan saw then that Charlotte had a syringe in her hand. She watched as the other girl first dabbed a spot with iodine, then neatly punctured the skin of the sick man's arm. Mrs McQuarrie came hurrying back carrying a tray on which were a bottle of brandy, a jug of water and a glass. Charlotte poured the brandy and water into the glass, and then while his wife and Susan held the boss in position Charlotte put the glass to his lips. Susan observed with thankfulness that the colour of his face was now almost normal and his eyes were open.

"He will be all right now," Charlotte said as she smiled down into her patient's face; then she glanced at Susan. "Thank you," she said, and the latter knew that she had been dismissed politely but firmly from the sickroom. Susan returned to the dining room and saw that Milton and Melissa were still there.

"Thought I'd better wait a while," Milton explained. "Just in case I was needed for anything. How's the boss?"

"Nurse says he'll be all right now," Susan said, and looked at the other two. The same thought was in all their minds, she knew. Would there be another attack?

"I didn't have time to tell Mrs Mac this morning," Milton went on, "but there was a message from Ian; he's on his way back."

"Oh, good!" said Susan. "That'll be a relief to her."

At that same moment Mrs McQuarrie came into the room and Milton gave her the message from Ian.

"Oh, good," she said, echoing Susan's words. She glanced at the table, then at Melissa. "Well, if everyone's finished——" she paused for a moment, "we must just carry on as usual. The boss is—over it, and he couldn't be in better hands than Charlotte's. Melissa, you just stay in this morning in case you're wanted. And Susan, could you get a message through to Alan before your school starts?"

Susan glanced at her wrist watch. "Of course," she said. "I'll go over now. What's the message?"

"Just to get back as soon as possible," Mrs McQuarrie said briefly. "Charlotte thinks he should."

As Susan hurried down the steps and along the covered way to the schoolroom her thoughts turned to Ian and his impending return. Her heart gave a kind of leap at the thought that she would soon be seeing him. 'It's seemed a long time,' she thought, and an even longer time since they had talked together. Really talked, as friends—perhaps even more than that. Then she thought of Letty French and of the evening when she had seen her with Ian on the veranda. Susan hurried into the schoolroom. It was early, and she should be able to get her message over without much trouble. She switched on the set and swung the front lever over. Almost at once a voice came through. "This is the Royal Flying Doctor Base at Alice Springs. Can I help you? Over."

"This is Kanoch Doon Homestead speaking," Susan replied. "Call sign XXV 3. Would you please ask Dr Alan McQuarrie to return as soon as possible as his father is not so well. Over."

Before the children came trooping in Susan had just time to dash up to the house to tell Mrs McQuarrie that the message had been sent. The morning seemed very long to her. Even though it was the morning for the nature study lesson which she enjoyed as much as the children. To-day the teacher was talking about goannas and lizards, their habitats and habits. Normally Susan would have been hanging on every word and checking up with the various pictures and diagrams mentioned, but to-day she found it very difficult to concentrate.

"I know where there's a goanna nest," Michael said at the end of the lesson. "Want to see it, Miss Susan?"

"I know where there's a mallee fowl's mound," Josephine put in. "One of the abo stockmen showed it to me. Want to—?"

"Yes, but not now," Susan said. "Now, I think it would be a very good idea if you sat at your desks and wrote out in your own words all you can remember of what the teacher told you."

"Knew it all anyway," boasted James. "Could we make it into a story?" and Hilary asked eagerly,

"Yes, and could we make some drawings of it?"

Susan nodded. "All right," she said. "What about making up a story about a family of goannas, giving them names, and making little sketches as you go on? James, give out the books, please."

All the time Susan was talking to the children her ears were strained for the sound of an approaching car or plane. 'Who will be the first to arrive?' she wondered. "Ian or Alan? Oh, I do hope the boss is really better and that there'll be no more attacks. What a good thing Charlotte was here!' She looked around at the busy little class in front of her and smiled at the intent faces.

Lunch break arrived at last. Susan dismissed the children and hurried up to the house. It was very quiet up there, but when she passed through the dining room and peeped into the kitchen she saw that Mrs McQuarrie and Melissa were in there preparing lunch as usual.

"It's cold lunch to-day, Susan," Mrs McQuarrie said over her shoulder as she went on shredding lettuce. "Ham and beef with salad, followed by fruit and cream."

"Sounds delicious. How's the boss?"

"He's doing fine. Charlotte's with him." She turned and looked at Susan. "That girl's as good as a doctor any day. I'm just wondering if we ought to have sent for Alan, as he was coming to-morrow anyway. However, it was Charlotte's decision and she ought to know."

"Oh, yes, I'm sure she knows what she's doing," Susan agreed reassuringly, and Mrs McQuarrie nodded and turned again to the pile of lettuce and tomatoes on the table.

Susan drew a breath of relief.

"Has—anyone arrived yet?" she asked, trying to make her voice sound casual.

"No, not yet," but even as Mrs McQuarrie spoke they all heard the sound of the jeep in the distance but coming rapidly nearer. "Good, that'll be Ian," Mrs McQuarrie said, laying down her knife and hurrying out on to the veranda.

Susan's heart was beginning to beat hard and fast and she knew that there was a tell-tale flush in her cheeks. Melissa looked at her teasingly and grinned.

"Seemed a long time, hasn't it?" she remarked, and Susan's face became even more heated. They heard the vehicle stop, and then Ian's voice greeting his mother. Then followed a long, low-voiced murmuring, and presently Mrs McQuarrie returned, followed by Ian.

"Hello, girls," he said, smiling impartially at them both, "how's things?" He turned again to his mother. "But how's Dad now?"

"Better," she said. "Much better, and he's got a wonderful nurse looking after him." Susan saw her give her son a long considering look before turning away. "Look, let's have lunch now, and I can give you all the news while we're having it. Susan, I've told Melissa to give you and the children their lunch here in the kitchen just for to-day. You understand, don't you?"

"Why, of course, Auntie Mac," Susan said, avoiding Ian's eye, though she could not have said why. "I understand. I'll call the children in now," and she turned and went quickly from the room. Her heart was racing and she had to clench her hands to stop them from trembling. Oh, why was Ian so casual now? she thought despairingly.

Alan arrived in the middle of the afternoon just as Susan had finished school. Melissa came into her room as she was preparing to take her usual shower after the ~~day's activities. She~~ looked excited and began at once,

"Sue, I've been talking with Alan. Did *you* know—about Charlotte, I mean?"

Susan looked at her and nodded. "Yes," she said. "He told me when I was at Alice Springs."

"So that was what the row was about. You know, I often used to wonder. It seemed to go on and on, and get worse and worse. Well—" she paused and looked at Susan with eyes bright with curiosity, "I wonder what the boss thinks of Charlotte now."

"Does he—er—perhaps he doesn't recognise her," Susan suggested, watching Melissa's face.

"He didn't," she agreed. "But Alan told him."

"Told him?" Susan stared at the younger girl. "Goodness, what did the boss say, Melissa?"

"Well," she gave an excited giggle, "I don't know whether his illness has softened him up, or whether he's been doing some thinking over the last few years, but Alan said he just nodded and remarked that Charlotte was a fine lass."

"Well!" Susan looked at Melissa, then said, "D'you know, I don't believe that either of your reasons is correct. No, I think it was Charlotte herself. She's the kind of girl that very few men could resist. She's been nursing him, too—and you know what they say about nurses."

"Ministering angel, and all that sort of thing?" Melissa enquired. "You could be right, Sue. It's real bonzer, isn't it? Now, how about you and Ian?"

"Nothing to report," Susan said, laughing in spite of herself.

"Well, anyway, Letty's off the map," said Melissa. "I met her only a couple of days ago and she never mentioned Ian, or even sent any fond messages about seeing him—not like Letty. I guess even she's had enough; maybe there's someone else around."

"I wonder," Susan said lightly.

"Don't wonder too long," Melissa advised, strolling to the door. "See you later!"

Susan found herself dressing with extra care that evening. But just as she was almost ready to go up for the evening meal, she had another visitor—Alan.

"Can I come in?" he called.

"Why, hello, Alan," Susan greeted him, looking at him in some surprise. "Sit down." She thought he looked rather ill at ease, and wondered why.

"Look, Sue," he began abruptly, sitting down on the edge of the chair, "I—I feel I owe you an apology." Susan sat down opposite and waited. "It—er—concerns Ian. I—er—" he moved restlessly, "well, what I mean is—you and Ian were getting on very well—" He looked across at Susan, but she said nothing. "Well—" he said again, "did I spoil things between you?" Then as she still said nothing, "I feel an awful swine, Sue. I—I did deliberately try to—Oh, lord, this is awful, but you see, I—I hadn't met Charlotte again, and—"

"Oh, please, Alan—" Susan interrupted suddenly. She got up from her chair and went to the window. "I—I don't know what you're talking about, so shut up, will you?"

Alan looked at her averted face and muttered uncomfortably, "Well, you see, Sue, it's Ma. She's been telling me about you and Ian, and that—something seems to have gone wrong. She likes you, Sue—" His voice trailed away, then started up again. "Look, shall I talk to Ian? I—"

"No!" She swung round and faced him with flaming cheeks and flashing eyes. "Certainly not. Alan, this is my business, so please don't interfere, and there's nothing for you to worry about."

"O.K., O.K.," he said soothingly. There was a short silence, then Alan said, "It's O.K., Sue, about Dad and Charlotte. He—"

"Yes, I know," Susan said. "Melissa told me. It's grand news, Alan. What about you and Ian?"

He rose to his feet and smiled at her. "That's O.K. too. I—I told him everything, but I think you were right; he'd guessed quite a lot. Well," he threw an affectionate arm round her shoulders, "thanks for everything, Sue. Coming over?"

As they paced slowly over to the house, Alan said, "Here's another piece of news, Sue. Melissa told Ma that she and Milton want to be engaged. Romance is certainly in the air at Kanoch Doon."

Susan burst out laughing. "I shall never be able to keep up with Melissa's plans," she said. "First she was going to be a teacher, then she was determined to be a vet, and now—a housewife!"

Alan laughed with her.

"She's just a kid," he said. "Anyway, Ma has told them that Melissa must wait till she's eighteen, that's in three months' time, and Milton till he has finished his apprenticeship—another six months. Then—" he laughed again, "we shall see. Dad's looking fine, and we're allowing him up this evening for an hour. He's accepted the fact that he has to take things easy from now on. I think this morning's do scared him quite a bit."

Susan nodded, and as she followed Alan up the steps of the big front veranda, they saw that Douglas

McQuarrie was already there, stretched out in a chaise-longue with cushions at his head and back. Susan thought he looked remarkably well compared with his condition of the morning. Charlotte was beside him and they were smiling at each other.

"Hello, Susan," he called, and she crossed the veranda to his side. "I'm nothing but an old fraud, sitting here like a V.I.P."

"But that's what you are," she said, sitting down beside him, "and it's wonderful to see you looking so much better—and out of bed, too."

"Aye, but it's not for long, I'm afraid." He raised his hands, then let them drop to his lap. "These women! Only up for an hour, so says my pretty nurse, backed up of course by my wife."

"Well, I expect they know best," said Susan. He smiled and agreed with her, and she was struck by the look of peace on his face; as if a battle had been fought and won against his own narrow, unrelenting nature.

"Tea's ready!" Mrs McQuarrie called from the door, and Susan saw that Ian was in the dining room with her. Charlotte went in and brought a tray out for the boss, and everyone else trooped into the dining room. During the meal Susan stole one or two glances in Ian's direction. Once she caught his eye and he smiled and nodded. Her spirits rose with a bound and she began to wonder again how she could manage to get him to herself. But afterwards on the veranda, and without any manoeuvring on her part, she found him beside her.

"Well, how are you, Sue?" he asked, and she looked at him in slight surprise. There seemed to be a real look of concern in his blue eyes and she began to wonder if she looked ill, or tired. But he was here beside her, and for the moment that was enough.

"I'm fine, thank you, Ian," she said. "How are you?"

"Oh, I'm all right," he said, and Susan became even more puzzled, for his tone seemed to imply that though he was all right, she was not. Susan looked across the veranda. Douglas McQuarrie had gone obediently back to his room and Alan and Charlotte had gone with him. Melissa and Milton were sitting on the top veranda step and were plainly absorbed in each other.

"Well—" Ian began, and at that moment his mother came out on to the veranda and looked down at him and Susan. She smiled in a contented way.

"It's a lovely night, Ian," she said. "Why don't you and Susan take a little walk?" But almost before she had finished speaking Ian shot to his feet.

"Sorry, Ma," he said briskly, "but I've got business down at the men's quarters. Susan will excuse me, I'm sure."

Mrs McQuarrie looked at him and shrugged her shoulders as she went back into the house; but Susan also rose to her feet. Her face was flushed, but there was a determined look about the set of her lips.

"I'll walk down with you," she said to Ian. "It's on my way," and she followed him down the veranda steps. Now that Susan had made up her mind she wasted no time; for this, she felt, was her opportunity.

"Ian," she began, stepping beside him and looking up into his face, "what's the matter? I—I thought we were friends, but it's years, at least it seems like that, since you even spoke to me—alone, I mean." She paused, her breath seeming to catch in her throat.

Ian's steps slowed down slightly, then he said quite casually, "You're imagining things, aren't you? After all, so much has happened lately, and I've been away with the mustering and the cattle sales, and you at the Alice. And then there's been Dad's illness, and—Alan and Charlotte's engagement." He paused for a moment, then added, "I guess things'll settle down now into the old routine."

There was a silence and Susan could almost feel Ian drawing away from her, but having started she was determined to force an issue. She knew that she could not go on like this.

"Well, I do hope so," she said at last, then added, "Ian, I—I miss our evening rides and walks." She stole an anxious glance at his face, but could read nothing from it. He slightly increased his pace, but Susan followed. 'Well, what now?' she asked herself despairingly. 'If you can't get him to talk now you never will, and you know that your whole life and happiness depends on it.'

"Oh, Ian," she burst out, and grasped his arm, "please, please tell me what's gone wrong between us. I—I thought you—liked me, quite a lot, but now—please won't you—?"

"Very well." His tone was rough as he stopped and faced her. "If you insist, Sue, I'll tell you, and don't think I'm not sorry for you. I am." His voice was suddenly gentle as he looked down into her startled face.

"Sorry for me?" Susan echoed on a high note, "But I just don't understand what you mean." But in spite of her perplexity she was conscious of a feeling of triumph, for she had at least made him open up.

"I think you know quite well what I mean," Ian said. "So why pretend? As I said before, I'm sorry that you've been let down, but—"

"Let down?" she interrupted. "Oh, please don't worry about letting me down, and there's no need to feel sorry if—if you have found that you—you made a mistake."

He turned and stared at her.

"I'd very much like to know how *I* have let you down," he said. "I've never given you any reason to think that—well—"

Susan's face was crimson now and there were tears of humiliation in her eyes.

"But I thought we were friends," she interrupted desperately. "That's all I meant, Ian. I—just can't understand why we're not friends—any longer." Her heart was like a heavy load in her breast. Had she made a terrible mistake about Ian? Had she misunderstood a friendly interest for something much deeper? She had thought that the coolness between herself and Ian was due to his wrong ideas about Alan. But was it? She had a sudden urge to rush away from him; to her room, anywhere, just to hide her face. But then she drew a deep trembling breath and knew, whatever the outcome, she *had* to know.

"We still are friends, I hope," she heard Ian say in that maddeningly-calm voice of his. "Now—" he looked about him and Susan saw that they were nearing the men's quarters, "I'm afraid I must—"

"No!" she said sharply, urgently. "Look, Ian, I'm sorry if I've made a—mistake about—us. I wish I could—" she stared up into his face and he looked down and suddenly caught her by the shoulders.

"Sue," he said in a low voice, "you're—crying. Why? You—look, girl—" he added roughly, and almost pushed her away from him, "no chap likes to be—second-best. There now, you've got it, so—"

"Second—?" Susan stared up at him with tear-bright eyes, but felt that the awful load in her breast was miraculously eased. "Oh, Ian, I—second-best, did you say? I—" she drew a deep breath. "I—suppose you mean Alan?" Ian nodded without looking at her. "But, Ian, I knew about Charlotte from the first—Alan himself told me. He also told me about the quarrel and how it all started. He—he asked my advice; he was very unhappy. Oh, Ian, don't you see, Alan has never been more to me than a friend. It's you—you, Ian, and always has been."

He stared down once more into her face.

"D'you know what you're saying?" he said. "You're implying that—"

"I'm not implying anything," Susan said with an unsteady laugh, "I'm telling you that I love you!"

He stared down into her face. Then his arms went round her, and she felt his lips hard upon hers.

"Sue, my darling," he whispered, "I love you, too. I guess I loved you from the moment I saw you, but—"

She sighed and whispered softly, "But what, Ian?"

He stroked the dark hair away from her eyes.

"Darling, have you thought, really thought of what your life will be now, here on a cattle station, year after year? There's not much change or variety, you know. You're from the Old Country. Don't you think that, as time goes on, you'll miss all sorts of things you've been used to? I'd hate to see you unhappy and—"

"Don't talk such rubbish," Susan interrupted. "I'm not a child, and I know what I want. Darling, places don't really matter. It's the people that count. What I mean is, to live with the person you love makes a home, doesn't matter where it is. See?" She smiled up into his eyes, and felt the hard pressure of his arms around her.

"You're a wise little person, Sue," he said.

She looked around her, at the wide paddocks, the distant hills, and thought that everything looked different all at once. The hills were bathed in a more than usually golden light; the sudden call of a galah sounded sweet and melodious all at once, and as she looked over her shoulder at the gleaming white of Kanoch Doon it looked to her like—home.

"Darling Ian," she said, and raised her lips again to his, "I'm so—happy."

There followed a blissful silence, then Ian said, "Mum—and the boss will be pleased about this. They've wanted me to settle down for ages now."

Susan looked up at him, then started to laugh. "D'you know something?" she said. "I don't know how I'm going to live up to you, darling; you're *so* romantic."

Ian looked down into her dancing eyes, then grinned sheepishly. "Well, you should know me by now," he said. "I'm just an ordinary plain cattleman."

"Not plain at all," Susan smiled. "You've got *beautiful* blue eyes. I think it was your eyes that I first—"

"We're wasting time," Ian interrupted, laughing; then his voice changed and the clasp of his arms tightened round her. "Kiss me, my darling," he murmured.

Each month from Harlequin

8 NEW FULL LENGTH ROMANCE NOVELS

Listed below are the last three months' releases:

1857 CRUISE TO A WEDDING, Betty Neels
1858 ISLAND OF DARKNESS, Rebecca Stratton
1859 THE MAN OUTSIDE, Jane Donnelly
1860 HIGH-COUNTRY WIFE, Gloria Bevan
1861 THE STAIRWAY TO ENCHANTMENT, Lucy Gillen
1862 CHATEAU IN PROVENCE, Rozella Lake
1863 McCABE'S KINGDOM, Margaret Way
1864 DEAR TYRANT, Margaret Malcolm
1865 STRANGER IN THE GLEN, Flora Kidd
1866 THE GREATER HAPPINESS, Katrina Britt
1867 FLAMINGO FLYING SOUTH, Joyce Dingwell
1868 THE DREAM ON THE HILL, Lilian Peake
1869 THE HOUSE OF THE EAGLES, Elizabeth Ashton
1870 TO TRUST MY LOVE, Sandra Field
1871 THE BRAVE IN HEART, Mary Burchell
1872 CINNAMON HILL, Jan Andersen
1873 A PAVEMENT OF PEARL, Iris Danbury
1874 DESIGN FOR DESTINY, Sue Peters
1875 A PLUME OF DUST, Wynne May
1876 GATE OF THE GOLDEN GAZELLE, Dorothy Cork
1877 MEANS TO AN END, Lucy Gillen
1878 ISLE OF DREAMS, Elizabeth Dawson
1879 DARK VIKING, Mary Wibberley
1880 SWEET SUNDOWN, Margaret Way

PLEASE NOTE: All Harlequin Romances from #1857 onward are 75c. Books below that number, where available are priced at 60c through Harlequin Reader Service until December 31st, 1975.

These titles are available at your local bookseller, or through the Harlequin Reader Service, M.P.O. Box 707, Niagara Falls, N.Y. 14302; Canadian address 649 Ontario St., Stratford, Ont.

Have You Missed Any of These Harlequin Romances?

- ☐ 427 NURSE BROOKES
  Kate Norway
- ☐ 438 MASTER OF SURGERY
  Alex Stuart
- ☐ 446 TO PLEASE THE DOCTOR
  Marjorie Moore
- ☐ 458 NEXT PATIENT, DOCTOR
  ANNE, Elizabeth Gilzean
- ☐ 468 SURGEON OF DISTINCTION
  Mary Burchell
- ☐ 469 MAGGY, Sara Seale
- ☐ 486 NURSE CARIL'S NEW POST
  Caroline Trench
- ☐ 487 THE HAPPY ENTERPRISE
  Eleanor Farnes
- ☐ 491 NURSE TENNANT
  Elizabeth Hoy
- ☐ 494 LOVE IS MY REASON
  Mary Burchell
- ☐ 495 NURSE WITH A DREAM
  Norrey Ford
- ☐ 503 NURSE IN CHARGE
  Elizabeth Gilzean
- ☐ 504 PETER RAYNAL, SURGEON
  Marjorie Moore

- ☐ 584 VILLAGE HOSPITAL
  Margaret Malcolm
- ☐ 599 RUN AWAY FROM LOVE
  Jean S. Macleod
  (Original Harlequin title
  "Nurse Companion")
- ☐ 631 DOCTOR'S HOUSE
  Dorothy Rivers
- ☐ 647 JUNGLE HOSPITAL
  Juliet Shore
- ☐ 672 GREGOR LOTHIAN, SURGEON
  Joan Blair
- ☐ 683 DESIRE FOR THE STAR
  Averil Ives
  (Original Harlequin title
  "Doctor's Desire")
- ☐ 744 VERENA FAYRE, PROBA-
  TIONER, Valerie K. Nelson
- ☐ 745 TENDER NURSE, Hilda Nickson
- ☐ 757 THE PALM-THATCHED
  HOSPITAL, Juliet Shore
- ☐ 758 HELPING DOCTOR MEDWAY
  Jan Haye
- ☐ 764 NURSE ANN WOOD
  Valerie K. Nelson

PLEASE NOTE: All Harlequin Romances from #1857 onwards are 75c. Books below that number, **where available are priced at 60c** through Harlequin Reader Service until December 31st, 1975.

TO: HARLEQUIN READER SERVICE, Dept. N 506
M.P.O. Box 707, Niagara Falls, N.Y. 14302
Canadian address: Stratford, Ont., Canada

☐ Please send me the free Harlequin Romance Catalogue.
☐ Please send me the titles checked.

I enclose $________ (No C.O.D.'s). All books listed are 60c each. To help defray postage and handling cost, please add 25c.

Name ______________________________

Address ____________________________

City/Town __________________________

State/Prov. ___________________ Zip __________

AA-1